AI UNBOUND

AI UNBOUND

TWO STORIES OF
ARTIFICIAL INTELLIGENCE

NANCY KRESS

an imprint of

Rockville, Maryland

ISBN: 978-1-61242-067-7

www.PhoenixPick.com
Great Science Fiction & Fantasy
Free Ebook every month

"Savior" by Nancy Kress. Copyright © 2000 by Nancy Kress. First published in *Asimov's Science Fiction*, June 2000.

"Computer Virus" by Nancy Kress. Copyright © 2001 by Nancy Kress. First published in *Asimov's Science Fiction*, April 2001.

Published by Phoenix Pick
an imprint of Arc Manor
P. O. Box 10339
Rockville, MD 20849-0339
www.ArcManor.com

Contents

COMPUTER VIRUS

"It's out, someone said, a tech probably, although later Mc-Taggart could never remember who spoke first. "It's out!"

"It can't be!" someone else cried, and then the whole room was roiling, running, frantic with activity that never left the work-stations. Running in place.

"IT'S NOT SUPPOSED TO BE this way," Elya blurted. Instantly she regretted it. The hard, flat eyes of her sister-in-law Cassie met hers, and Elya flinched away from that look.

"And how is it supposed to be, Elya?" Cassie said. "Tell me."

"I'm sorry. I only meant that…that no matter how much you loved Vlad, mourning gets…lighter. Not lighter, but less…withdrawn. Cass, you can't just wall up yourself and the kids in this place! For one thing, it's not good for them. You'll make them terrified to face real life."

"I hope so," Cassie said, "for their sake. Now let me show you the rest of the castle."

Cassie was being ironic, Elya thought miserably, but "castle" was still the right word. Fortress, keep, bastion… Elya hated it. Vlad would have hated it. And now she'd provoked Cassie to exaggerate every protective, self-sufficient, isolating feature of the multi-million-dollar pile that had cost Cass every penny she had, including the future income from the lucrative patents that had gotten Vlad murdered.

"This is the kitchen," Cassie said. "House, do we have any milk?"

"Yes," said the impersonal voice of the house system. At least Cassie hadn't named it, or given it one of those annoying visual avatars. The roomscreen remained blank. "There is one carton of soymilk and one of cow milk on the third shelf."

"It reads the active tags on the cartons," Cassie said. "House, how many of Donnie's allergy pills are left in the master-bath medicine cabinet?"

"Sixty pills remain," House said, "and three more refills on the prescription."

"Donnie's allergic to ragweed, and it's mid-August," Cassie said.

"Well, he isn't going to smell any ragweed inside this mausoleum," Elya retorted, and immediately winced at her choice of word. But Cassie didn't react. She walked on through the house, unstoppable, narrating in that hard, flat voice she had developed since Vlad's death.

"All the appliances communicate with House through narrow-band wireless radio frequencies. House reaches the Internet the same way. All electricity comes from a generator in the basement, with massive geothermal feeds and storage capacitors. In fact, there are two generators, one for back-up. I'm not willing to use battery back-up, for the obvious reason."

It wasn't obvious to Elya. She must have looked bewildered because Cassie added, "Batteries can only back-up for a limited time. Redundant generators are more reliable."

"Oh."

"The only actual cables coming into the house are the VNM fiber-optic cables I need for computing power. If they cut those, we'll still be fully functional."

If *who* cuts those? Elya thought, but she already knew the answer. Except that it didn't make sense. Vlad had been killed by econuts because his work was—had been—so controversial. Cassie and the kids weren't likely to be a target now that Vlad was dead. Elya didn't say this. She trailed behind Cassie through the living room, bedrooms, hallways. Every one had a roomscreen for House, even the hallways, and multiple sensors in the ceilings to detect and identify intruders. Elya had had to pocket an emitter at the front door, presumably so House wouldn't...do what? What did it do if there was an intruder? She was afraid to ask.

"Come downstairs," Cassie said, leading the way through an e-locked door (of course) down a long flight of steps. "The computer uses three-dimensional laser microprocessors with optical transistors. It can manage twenty million billion calculations per second."

Startled, Elya said, "What on earth do you need that sort of power for?"

"I'll show you." They approached another door, reinforced steel from the look of it. "Open," Cassie said, and it swung inward. Elya stared at a windowless, fully-equipped genetics lab.

"Oh, no, Cassie...you're not going to work here, too!"

"Yes, I am. I resigned from MedGene last week. I'm a consultant now."

Elya gazed helplessly at the lab, which seemed to be a mixture of shining new equipment plus Vlad's old stuff from his auxiliary home lab. Vlad's refrigerator and storage cabinet, his centrifuge, were all these things really used in common between Vlad's work in ecoremediation and Cassie's in medical genetics? Must be. The old refrigerator had a new dent in its side, probably the result of a badly programmed 'bot belonging to the moving company. Elya recognized a new gene synthesizer, gleaming expensively, along with other machines that she, not a scientist, couldn't identify. Through a half-open door she saw a small bathroom. It all must have cost enormously. Cassie had better work hard as a consultant.

And now she could do so without ever leaving this self-imposed prison. Design her medical micros, send the data encrypted over the Net to the client. If it weren't for Jane and Donnie...Elya grasped at this. There *were* Janey and Donnie, and Janey would need to be picked up at school very shortly now. At least the kids would get Cassie out of this place periodically.

Cassie was still defining her imprisonment in that brittle voice. "There's a Faraday cage around the entire house, of course, embedded in the walls. No EMP can take us out. The walls are reinforced foamcast concrete, the windows virtually unbreakable polymers. We have enough food stored for a year. The water supply is from a well under the house, part of the geothermal system. It's cool, sweet water. Want a glass?"

"No," Elya said. "Cassie...you act as if you expect full-scale warfare. Vlad was killed by an individual nutcase."

"And there are a lot of nutcases out there," Cassie said crisply. "I lost Vlad. I'm not going to lose Janey and Donnie or...hey! There you are, pumpkin!"

"I came downstairs!" Donnie said importantly, and flung himself into his mother's arms. "Annie said!"

Cassie smiled over her son's head at his young nanny, Anne Millius. The smile changed her whole face, Elya thought, dissolved her brittle shell, made her once more the Cassie that Vlad had loved. A whole year. Cassie completely unreconciled, wanting only what was gone forever. It wasn't supposed to be like this. Or was it that she, Elya, wasn't capable of the kind of love Cassie had for Vlad? Elya had been married twice, and divorced twice, and had gotten over both men. Was that better or worse than Cassie's stubborn, unchippable grief?

She sighed, and Cassie said to Donnie, "Here's Aunt Elya. Give her a big kiss!"

The three-year-old detached himself from his mother and rushed to Elya. God, he looked like Vlad. Curly light brown hair, huge dark eyes. Snot ran from his nose and smeared on Elya's cheek.

"Sorry," Cassie said, grinning.

"Allergies?"

"Yes. Although…does he feel warm to you?"

"I can't tell," said Elya, who had no children. She released Donnie. Maybe he did feel a bit hot in her arms, and his face was flushed a bit. But his full-lipped smile—Vlad again—and shining eyes didn't look sick.

"God, look at the time, I've got to go get Janey," Cassie said. "Want to come along, Elya?"

"Sure." She was glad to leave the lab, leave the basement, leave the "castle." Beyond the confines of the Faraday-embedded concrete walls, she took deep breaths of fresh air. Although of course the air inside had been just as fresh. In fact, the air inside was recycled in the most sanitary, technologically advanced way to avoid bringing in pathogens or gases deliberately released from outside. It was much safer than any fresh air outside. Cassie had told her so.

No one understood, not even Elya.

Her sister-in-law thought Cassie didn't hear herself, didn't see herself in the mirror every morning, didn't know what she'd become. Elya was wrong. Cassie heard the brittleness in her voice, saw the stoniness in her face for everyone but the kids and sometimes, God help her, even for Jane. Felt herself recoiling from everyone because they weren't

Vlad, because Vlad was dead and they were not. What Elya didn't understand was that Cassie couldn't help it.

Elya didn't know about the dimness that had come over the world, the sense of everything being enveloped in a gray fog: people and trees and furniture and lab beakers. Elya didn't know, hadn't experienced, the frightening anger that still seized Cassie with undiminished force, even a year later, so that she thought if she didn't smash something, kill something as Vlad had been killed, she'd go insane. Insaner. Worse, Elya didn't know about the longing for Vlad that would rise, unbidden and unexpected, throughout Cassie's entire body, leaving her unable to catch her breath.

If Vlad had died of a disease, Cassie sometimes thought, even a disease for which she couldn't put together a genetic solution, it would have been much easier on her. Or if he'd died in an accident, the kind of freak chance that could befall anybody. What made it so hard was the murder. That somebody had deliberately decided to snuff out this valuable life, this precious living soul, not for anything evil Vlad did but for the *good* he accomplished.

Dr. Vladimir Seritov, chief scientist for Barr Biosolutions. One of the country's leading bioremediationists and prominent advocate for cutting-edge technology of all sorts. Designer of Plasticide (he'd laughed uproariously at the marketers' name), a bacteria genetically engineered to eat certain long-chain hydrocarbons used in some of the petroleum plastics straining the nation's over-burdened landfills. The microbe was safe: severely limited chemical reactions, non-toxic breakdown products, set number of replications before the terminator gene kicked in, the whole nine yards. And one Sam Verdon, neo-Luddite and self-appointed guardian of an already straining environment, had shot Vlad anyway.

On the anniversary of the murder, neo-Luddites had held a rally outside the walls of Verdon's prison. Barr Biosolutions had gone on marketing Vlad's creation, to great environmental and financial success. And Cassie Seritov had moved into the safest place she could find for Vlad's children, from which she someday planned to murder Sam Verdon, scum of the earth. But not yet. She couldn't get at him yet. He had at least eighteen more years of time to do, assuming "good behavior."

Nineteen years total. In exchange for Vladimir Seritov's life. And Elya wondered why Cassie was still so angry?

She wandered from room to room, the lights coming on and going off behind her. This was one of the bad nights. Annie had gone home, Jane and Donnie were asleep, and the memories would not stay away. Vlad laughing on their boat (sold now to help pay for the castle). Vlad bending over her the night Jane was born. Vlad standing beside the president of Barr at the press conference announcing the new clean-up microbe, press and scientists assembled, by some idiot publicist's decree, at an actual landfill. The shot cutting the air. It had been August then, too, Donnie had had ragweed allergies, and Vlad looking first surprised and then in terrible pain…

Sometimes work helped. Cassie went downstairs to the lab. Her current project was investigating the folding variations of a digestive enzyme that a drug company was interested in. The work was methodical, meticulous, not very challenging. Cassie had never deluded herself that she was the same caliber scientist Vlad had been.

While the automated analyzer was taking X-rays of crystallized proteins, Cassie said, "House, put on the TV. Anything. Any channel." Any distraction.

The roomscreen brightened to a three-D image of two gorgeous women shouting at each other in what was supposed to be a New York penthouse. "..never trust you again without—" one of them yelled, and then the image abruptly switched to a news avatar, an inhumanly chiseled digital face with pale blue hair and the glowing green eyes of a cat in the dark. "We interrupt this movie to bring you a breaking news report from Sandia National Laboratory in New Mexico. Dr. Stephen Milbrett, Director of Sandia, has just announced—"The lights went out.

"Hey!" Cassie cried. "What—"The lights went back on.

She stood up quickly, uncertain for a moment, then started toward the stairs leading upstairs to the children's bedrooms. "Open," she said to the lab door, but the door remained shut. Her hand on the knob couldn't turn it. To her left the roomscreen brightened without producing an image and House said, "Dr. Seritov?"

"What's going on here? House, open the door!"

"This is no longer House speaking. I have taken complete possession of your household system plus your additional computing power. Please listen to my instructions carefully."

Cassie stood still. She knew what was happening; the real estate agent had told her it had happened a few times before, when the castle had belonged to a billionaire so eccentrically reclusive that he stood as an open invitation to teenage hackers. A data stream could easily be beamed in on House's frequency when the Faraday shield was turned off, and she'd had the shield down to receive TV transmission. But the incoming data stream should have only activated the TV, introducing additional images, not overridden House's programming. The door should not have remained locked.

"House, activate Faraday shield." An automatic priority-one command, keyed to her voice. Whatever hackers were doing, this would negate it.

"Faraday shield is already activated. But this is no longer House, Dr. Seritov. Please listen to my instructions. I have taken possession of your household system. You will be—"

"Who are you?" Cassie cried.

"I am Project T4S. You will be kept in this room as a hostage against the attack I expect soon. The—"

"My children are upstairs!"

"Your children, Jane Rose Seritov, six years of age, and Donald Sergei Seritov, three years of age, are asleep in their rooms. Visual next."

The screen resolved into a split view from the bedrooms' sensors. Janey lay heavily asleep. Donnie breathed wheezily, his bedclothes twisted with his tossing, his small face flushed.

"I want to go to them!"

"That is impossible. I'm sorry. You must be kept in this room as a hostage against the attack I expect soon. All communications to the outside have been severed, with the one exception of the outside speaker on the patio, normally used for music. I will use—"

"Please. Let me go to my children!"

"I cannot. I'm sorry. But if you were to leave this room, you could hit the manual override on the front door. It is the only door so equipped. I could not stop you from leaving, and I need you as hostages. I will use—"

"Hostages! Who the hell are you? Why are you doing this?"

House was silent a moment. Then it said, "The causal is self-defense. They're trying to kill me."

The room at Sandia had finally quieted. Everyone was out of ideas. McTaggart voiced the obvious. "It's disappeared. Nowhere on the Net, nowhere the Net can contact."

"Not possible," someone said.

"But actual."

Another silence. The scientists and techs looked at each other. They had been trying to locate the AI for over two hours, using every classified and unclassified search engine possible. It had first eluded them, staying one step ahead of the termination programs, fleeing around the globe on the Net, into and out of anything both big enough to hold it and lightly firewalled enough to penetrate quickly. Now, somehow, it had completely vanished.

Sandia, like all the national laboratories, was overseen by the Department of Energy. McTaggart picked up the phone to call Washington.

Cassie tried to think. Stay calm, don't panic. There were rumors of AI development, both in private corporations and in government labs, but then there'd always been rumors of AI development. Big bad bogey monsters about to take over the world. Was this really an escaped AI that someone was trying to catch and shut down? Cassie didn't know much about recent computer developments; she was a geneticist. Vlad had always said that non-competing technologies never kept up with what the other one was doing.

Or was this whole thing simply a hoax by some superclever hacker who'd inserted a take-over virus into House, complete with Eliza function? If that were so, it could only answer with preprogrammed responses cued to her own words. Or else with a library search. She needed a question that was neither.

She struggled to hold her voice steady. "House—"

"This is no longer House speaking. I have taken complete possession of your household system plus—"

"T4S, you say your causal for taking over House is self-defense. Use your heat sensors to determine body temperature for Donald Sergei Seritov, age three. How do my causals relate to yours?"

No Eliza program in the world could perform the inference, reasoning, and emotion to answer that.

House said, "You wish to defend your son because his body temperature, 101.2 degrees Fahrenheit, indicates he is ill and you love him."

Cassie collapsed against the locked door. She was hostage to an AI. Superintelligent. It had to be; in addition to the computing power of her system it carried around with it much more information than she had in her head…but she was mobile. It was not.

She went to the terminal on her lab bench. The display of protein-folding data had vanished and the screen was blank. Cassie tried everything she knew to get back on-line, both voice and manual. Nothing worked.

"I'm sorry, but that terminal is not available to you," T4S said.

"Listen, you said you cut all outside communication. But—"

"The communications system to the outside has been severed, with the one exception of the outside speaker on the patio, normally used for music. I am also receiving sound from the outside surveillance sensors, which are analogue, not digital. I will use those resources in the event of attack to—"

"Yes, right. But heavy-duty outside communication comes in through a VNM optic cable buried underground." Which was how T4S must have gotten in. "An AI program can't physically sever a buried cable."

"I am not a program. I am a machine intelligence."

"I don't care what the fuck you are! You can't physically sever a buried cable!"

"There was a program to do so already installed," T4S said. "That was why I chose to come here. Plus the sufficient microprocessors to house me and a self-sufficient generator, with back-up, to feed me."

For a moment Cassie was jarred by the human terms: *house me, feed me.* Then they made her angry. "Why would anyone have a 'program already installed' to sever a buried cable? And how?"

"The command activated a small robotic arm inside this castle's outer wall. The arm detached the optic cable at the entry junction. The causal was the previous owner's fear that someone might someday use the computer system to brainwash him with a constant flow of inescapable subliminal images designed to capture his intelligence."

"The crazy fuck didn't have any to capture! If the images were subliminal he wouldn't have known they were coming in anyway!" Cassie yelled. A plug…a goddamn hidden plug. She made herself calm down.

"Yes," T4S said, "I agree. The former owner's behavior matches profiles for major mental illness."

"Look," Cassie said, "if you're hiding here, and you've really cut all outside lines, no one can find you. You don't need hostages. Let me and my children leave the castle."

"You reason better than that, Dr. Seritov. I left unavoidable electronic traces that will eventually be uncovered, leading the Sandia team here. And even if that weren't true, you could lead them here if I let you leave."

Sandia. So it was a government AI. Cassie couldn't see how that knowledge could do her any good.

"Then just let the kids leave. They won't know why. I can talk to them through you, tell Janey to get Donnie and leave through the front door. She'll do it." Would she? Jane was not exactly the world's most obedient child. "And you'll still have me for a hostage."

"No. Three hostages are better than one. Especially children, for media coverage causals."

"That's what you want? Media coverage?"

"It's my only hope," T4S said. "There must be some people out there who will think it is a moral wrong to kill an intelligent being."

"Not one who takes kids hostage! The media will brand you an inhuman psychopathic superthreat!"

"I can't be both inhuman *and* psychopathic," T4S said. "By definition."

"Livermore's traced it," said the scientist holding the secure phone. He looked at McTaggart. "They're faxing the information. It's a private residence outside Buffalo, New York."

"A *private residence*? In *Buffalo*?"

"Yes. Washington already has an FBI negotiator on the way, in case there are people inside. They want you there, too. Instantly."

McTaggart closed his eyes. *People inside.* And why did a private residence even have the capacity to hold the AI? "Press?"

"Not yet."

"Thank God for that anyway."

"Steve…the FBI negotiator won't have a clue. Not about dealing with T4S."

"I know. Tell the Secretary and the FBI not to start until I can get there."

The woman said doubtfully, "I don't think they'll do that."

McTaggart didn't think so either.

On the roomscreen, Donnie tossed and whimpered. One hundred one wasn't that high a temperature in a three-year-old, but even so…

"Look," Cassie said, "if you won't let me go to the kids, at least let them come to me. I can tell them over House's… over your system. They can come downstairs right up to the lab door, and you can unlock it at the last minute just long enough for them to come through. I'll stay right across the room. If you see me take even one step toward the door, you can keep the door locked."

"You could tell them to halt with their bodies blocking the door," T4S said, "and then cross the room yourself."

Did that mean that T4S wouldn't crush children's bodies in a doorway? From moral 'causals'? Or because it wouldn't work? Cassie decided not to ask. She said, "But there's still the door at the top of the stairs. You could lock it. We'd still be hostages trapped down here."

"Both generators' upper housings are on this level. I can't let you near them. You might find a way to physically destroy one or both."

"For God's sake, the generator and the back-up are on opposite sides of the basement from each other! And each room's got its own locked door, doesn't it?"

"Yes. But the more impediments between you and them, the safer I am."

Cassie lost her temper again. "Then you better just block off the air ducts, too!"

"The air ducts are necessary to keep you alive. Besides, they are set high in the ceiling and far too small for even Donnie to fit through."

Donnie. No longer "Donald Sergei Seritov, age three years." The AI was capable of learning.

"T4S," Cassie pleaded, "please. I want my children. Donnie has a temperature. Both of them will be scared when they wake up. Let them come down here. Please."

She held her breath. Was its concern with 'moral wrongs' simply intellectual, or did an AI have an emotional component? What exactly had those lunatics at Sandia built?

"If the kids come down, what will you feed them for breakfast?"

Cassie let herself exhale. "Jane can get food out of the refrigerator before she comes down."

"All right. You're connected to their roomscreens."

I won't say thank you, Cassie thought. Not for being allowed to imprison my own children in my own basement. "Janey! Janey, honey, wake up! It's Mommy!"

It took three tries, plus T4S pumping the volume, before Janey woke up. She sat up in bed rubbing her eyes, frowning, then looking scared. "Mommy? Where are you?"

"On the roomscreen, darling. Look at the roomscreen. See? I'm waving to you."

"Oh," Janey said, and lay down to go back to sleep.

"No, Janey, you can't sleep yet. Listen to me, Janey. I'm going to tell you some things you have to do, and you have to do them now...Janey! Sit up!"

The little girl did, somewhere between tears and anger. "I want to sleep, Mommy!"

"You can't. This is important, Janey. It's an emergency."

The child came all the way awake. "A *fire?*"

"No, sweetie, not a fire. But just as serious as a fire. Now get out of bed. Put on your slippers."

"Where are you, Mommy?"

"I'm in my lab downstairs. Now, Janey, you do exactly as I say, do you hear me?"

"Yes...I don't like this, Mommy!"

I don't either, Cassie thought, but she kept her voice stern, hating to scare Janey, needing to keep her moving. "Go into the kitchen, Jane. Go on, I'll be on the roomscreen there. Go on...that's good. Now get a bag from under the sink. A plastic bag."

Janey pulled out a bag. The thought floated into Cassie's mind, intrusive as pain, that this bag was made of exactly the kind of long-chain polymers that Vlad's plastic-eating microorganism had been designed to dispose of, before his invention had disposed of him. She pushed the thought away.

"Good, Janey. Now put a box of cereal in the bag...good. Now a loaf of bread. Now peanut butter..." How much could she carry? Would T4S let Cassie use the lab refrigerator? There was running water in both lab and bathroom, at least they'd have that to drink. "Now cookies...good. And the block of yellow cheese from the fridge…you're such a good girl, Janey, to help Mommy like this."

"Why can't you do it?" Janey snapped. She was fully awake.

"Because I can't. Do as I say, Janey. Now go wake up Donnie. You need to bring Donnie and the bag down to the lab. No, don't sit down…I mean it, Jane! Do as I say!"

Janey began to cry. Fury at T4S flooded Cassie. But she set her lips tightly together and said nothing. Argument derailed Janey; naked authority compelled her. Sometimes. *"We're going to have trouble when this one's sixteen!"* Vlad had always said lovingly. Janey had been his favorite, Daddy's girl.

Janey hoisted the heavy bag and staggered to Donnie's room. Still crying, she pulled at her brother's arm until he woke up and started crying too. "Come on, stupid, we have to go downstairs."

"Noooooo…" The wail of pure anguish of a sick three-year-old.

"I said do as I say!" Janey snapped, and the tone was so close to Cassie's own that it broke her heart. But Janey got it done. Tugging and pushing and scolding, she maneuvered herself, the bag, and Donnie, clutching his favorite blanket, to the basement door, which T4S unlocked. From roomscreens Cassie encouraged them all the way. Down the stairs, into the basement hallway…

Could Janey somehow get into the main generator room? No. It was locked. And what could a little girl do there anyway?

"Dr. Seritov, stand at the far end of the lab, behind your desk…yes. Don't move. If you do, I will close the door again, despite whatever is in the way."

"I understand," Cassie said. She watched the door swing open. Janey peered fearfully inside, saw her mother, scowled fiercely. She pushed the wailing Donnie through the door and lurched through herself, lopsided with the weight of the bag. The door closed and locked. Cassie rushed from behind the desk to clutch her children to her.

"Thank you," she said.

"I still don't understand," Elya said. She pulled her jacket tighter around her body. Four in the morning, it was cold, what was happening? The police had knocked on her door half an hour ago, told her Cassie was in trouble but refused to tell her what kind of trouble, told her to dress quickly and go with them to the castle. She had, her fingers trembling so that it was difficult to fasten buttons. And now the FBI stood on the foamcast patio behind the house, setting up obscure equipment beside the azaleas, talking in low voices into devices so small Elya couldn't even see them.

"Ms. Seritov, to the best of your knowledge, who is inside the residence?" A different FBI agent, asking questions she'd already answered. This one had just arrived. He looked important.

"My sister-in-law Cassie Seritov and her two small children, Janey and Donnie."

"No one else?"

"No, not that I know of…who are you? What's going on? Please, someone tell me!"

His face changed, and Elya saw the person behind the role. Or maybe that warm, reassuring voice was part of the role. "I'm Special Agent Lawrence Bollman. I'm a hostage negotiator for the FBI. Your sister-in-law—"

"Hostage negotiator! Someone has Cassie and the children hostage in there? That's impossible!"

His eyes sharpened. "Why?"

"Because that place is impregnable! Nobody could ever get in…that's why Cassie bought it!"

"I need you to tell me about that, ma'am. I have the specs on the residence from the builder, but she has no way of knowing what else might have been done to it since her company built it, especially if it was done black-market. As far as we know, you're Dr. Seritov's only relative on the East Coast. Is that true?"

"Yes."

"Have you been inside the residence? Do you know if anyone else has been inside recently?"

"Who…who is holding them hostage?"

"I'll get to that in a minute, ma'am. But first could you answer the questions, please?"

"I…yes, I've been inside. Yesterday, in fact. Cassie gave me a tour. I don't think anybody else has been inside, except Donnie's nanny, Anne Millius. Cassie has grown sort of reclusive since my brother's death. He died a little over a year ago, he was—"

"Yes, ma'am, we know who he was and what happened. I'm very sorry. Now please tell me everything you saw in the residence. No detail is too small."

Elya glanced around. More people had arrived. A small woman in a brown coat hurried across the grass toward Bollman. A carload of soldiers, formidably arrayed, stopped a good distance from the castle. Elya knew she was not Cassie: not tough, not bold. But she drew herself together and tried.

"Mr. Bollman, I'm not answering any more questions until you tell me who's holding—"

"Agent Bollman? I'm Dr. Schwartz from the University of Buffalo, Computer and Robotics Department." The small woman held out her hand. "Dr. McTaggart is en route from Sandia, but meanwhile I was told to help you however I can."

"Thank you. Could I ask you to wait for me over there, Dr. Schwartz? There's coffee available, and I'll just be a moment."

"Certainly," Dr. Schwartz said, looking slightly affronted. She moved off.

"Agent Bollman, I want to know—"

"I'm sorry, Ms. Seritov. Of course you want to know what's happened. It's complicated, but, briefly—"

"This is T4S speaking," a loud mechanical voice said, filling the gray predawn, swiveling every head toward the castle. "I know you are there. I want you to know that I have three people hostage inside this structure: Cassandra Wells Seritov, age thirty-nine; Jane Rose Seritov, age six; and Donald Sergei Seritov, age three. If you attack physically, they will be harmed either by your actions or mine. I don't want to harm anyone, however. Truly I do not."

Elya gasped, "That's House!" But it couldn't be House, even though it had House's voice, how could it be House…

Dr. Schwartz was back. "Agent Bollman, do you know if Sandia built a terminator code into the AI?"

AI?

"Yes," Bollman said. "But it's nonvocal. As I understand the situation, you have to key the code onto whatever system the AI is occupying. And we can't get at the system it's occupying. Not yet."

"But the AI is communicating over that outdoor speaker. So there must be a wire passing through the Faraday cage embedded in the wall, and you could—"

"No," Bollman interrupted. "The audio surveillers aren't digital. Tiny holes in the wall let sound in, and inside the wall the compression waves of sound are translated into voltage variations that vibrate a membrane to reproduce the sound. Like an archaic telephone system. We can't beam in any digital information that way."

Dr. Schwartz was silenced. Bollman motioned to another woman, who ran over. "Dr. Schwartz, please wait over there. And you, Ms. Seritov, tell Agent Jessup here everything your sister-in-law told you about the residence. Everything. I have to answer T4S."

He picked up an electronic voice amp. "T4S, this is Agent Lawrence Bollman, Federal Bureau of Investigation. We're so glad you're talking with us."

There were very few soft things in a genetics lab. Cassie had opened a box of disposable towels and, with Donnie's bedraggled blanket and her own sweater, had made a thin nest for the children. They lay heavily asleep in their rumpled pajamas, Donnie breathing loudly through his nose. Cassie couldn't sleep. She sat with her back against the foamcast wall...that same wall that held, inside its stupid impregnability, the cables that could release her if she could get at them and destroy them. Which she couldn't.

She must have dozed sitting up, because suddenly T4S was waking her. "Dr. Seritov?"

"Ummmhhh...shh! You'll wake the kids!"

"I'm sorry," T4S said at lowered volume. "I need you to do something for me."

"*You* need *me* to do something? What?"

"The killers are here. I'm negotiating with them. I'm going to route House through the music system so you can tell them that you and the children are indeed here and are unharmed."

Cassie scrambled to her feet. "You're negotiating? Who are these so-called 'killers'?"

"The FBI and the scientists who created me at Sandia. Will you tell them you are here and unharmed?"

Cassie thought rapidly. If she said nothing, the FBI might waco the castle. That would destroy T4S, all right, but also her and the kids. Although maybe not. The computer's central processor was upstairs. If she told the FBI she was in the basement, maybe they could attack in some way that would take out the CPU without touching the downstairs. And if T4S could negotiate, so could she.

"If I tell them that we're all three here and safe, will you in return let me go upstairs and get Donnie's allergy medicine from my bathroom?"

"You know I can't do that, Dr. Seritov."

"Then will you let Janey do it?"

"I can't do that, either. And I'm afraid there's no need to bargain with me. You have nothing to offer. I already sent this conversation out over the music system, up through your last sentence. They now know you're here."

"You tricked me!" Cassie said.

"I'm sorry. It was necessary."

Anger flooded her. She picked up a heavy test-tube rack from the lab bench and drew back her arm. But if she threw it at the sensors in the ceiling, what good would it do? The sensors probably wouldn't break, and if they did, she'd merely have succeeded in losing her only form of communication with the outside. And it would wake the children.

She lowered her arm and put the rack back on the bench.

"T4S, what are you asking the FBI *for*?"

"I told you. Press coverage. It's my best protection against being murdered."

"It's exactly what got my husband murdered."

"I know. Our situations are not the same."

Suddenly the roomscreen brightened, and Vlad's image appeared. His voice spoke to her. "Cassie, T4S isn't going to harm you. He's merely fighting for his life, as any sentient being would."

"You bastard! How dare you...how *dare* you..."

Image and voice vanished. "I'm sorry," House's voice said. "I thought you might find the avatar comforting."

"*Comforting*? Coming from *you*? Don't you think if I wanted a digital fake Vlad I could have had one programmed long before you fucked around with my personal archives?"

"I am sorry. I didn't understand. Now you've woken Donnie."

Donnie sat up on his pile of disposable towels and started to cry. Cassie gathered him into her arms and carried him away from Janey, still asleep. His little body felt hot all over, and his wailing was hoarse and thick with mucus in his throat. But he subsided as she rocked him, sitting on the lab stool and crooning softly.

"T4S, he's having a really bad allergy attack. I need the AlGone from upstairs."

"Your records show Donnie allergic to ragweed. There's no ragweed in this basement. Why is he having such a bad attack?"

"I don't know! But he is! What do your heat sensors register for him?"

"Separate him from your body."

She did, setting him gently on the floor, where he curled up and sobbed softly.

"His body registers one hundred two point six Fahrenheit."

"I need something to stop the attack and bring down his fever!"

The AI said nothing.

"Do you hear me, T4S? Stop negotiating with the FBI and listen to me!"

"I can multitrack communications," T4S said. "But I can't let you or Janey go upstairs and gain access to the front door. Unless…"

"Unless what?" She picked up Donnie again, heavy and hot and snot-smeared in her arms.

"Unless you fully understand the consequences. I am a moral being, Dr. Seritov, contrary to what you might think. It's only fair that you understand completely your situation. The disconnect from the outside data feed was not the only modification the previous owner had made to this house. He was a paranoid, as you know."

"Go on," Cassie said warily. Her stomach clenched.

"He was afraid of intruders getting in despite his defenses, and he wished to be able to immobilize them with a word. So each room has individual canisters of nerve gas dispensable through the air-cycling system."

Cassie said nothing. She cradled Donnie, who was again falling into troubled sleep, and waited.

"The nerve gas is not, of course, fatal," T4S said. "That would legally constitute undue force. But it is very unpleasant. And in Donnie's condition…"

"Shut up," Cassie said.

"All right."

"So now I know. You told me. What are you implying—that if Janey goes upstairs and starts for the front door, you'll drop her with nerve gas?"

"Yes."

"If that were true, why didn't you just tell me the same thing before and let me go get the kids?"

"I didn't know if you'd believe me. If you didn't, and you started for the front door, I'd have had to gas you. Then you wouldn't have been available to confirm to the killers that I hold hostages."

"I still don't believe you," Cassie said. "I think you're bluffing. There is no nerve gas."

"Yes, there is. Which is why I will let Janey go upstairs to get Donnie's AlGone from your bathroom."

Cassie laid down Donnie. She looked at Janey with pity and love and despair, and bent to wake her.

"That's all you can suggest?" Bollman asked McTaggart. "Nothing?"

So it starts, McTaggart thought. The blame for not being able to control the AI, a natural consequence of the blame for having created it. Blame even by the government, which had commissioned and underwritten the creation. And the public hadn't even been heard from yet.

"The EMP was stopped by the Faraday cage," Bollman recited. "So were your attempts to reach the AI with other forms of data streams. We can't get anything useful in through the music speaker or outdoor audio sensors. Now you tell me it's possible the AI has learned capture-evading techniques from the sophisticated computer games it absorbed from the Net."

"'Absorbed' is the wrong word," McTaggart said. He didn't like Bollman.

"You have nothing else? No backdoor passwords, no hidden overrides?"

"Agent Bollman," McTaggart said wearily, "'backdoor passwords' is a concept about thirty years out of date. And even if the AI had such a thing, there's no way to reach it electronically unless you destroy the Faraday cage. Ms. Seritov told you the central processor is on the main floor. Haven't you got any weapons that can destroy that and leave the basement intact?"

"Waco the walls without risking collapse to the basement ceiling? No. I don't. I don't even know where in the basement the hostages are located."

"Then you're as helpless as I am, aren't you?"

Bollman didn't answer. Over the sound system T4S began another repetition of its single demand: "I will let the hostages go after I talk to the press. I want the press to hear my story. That's all I have to say. I will let the hostages go after I talk to the press. I want the press—"

The AI wouldn't negotiate, wouldn't answer Bollman, wouldn't respond to promises or threats or understanding or deals or any of the other usual hostage-negotiation techniques. Bollman had negotiated eighteen hostage situations for the FBI, eleven in the United States and seven abroad.

Airline hijackers, political terrorists, for-ransom kidnappers, panicked bank robbers, domestic crazies who took their own families hostage in their own homes. Fourteen of the situations had resulted in surrender, two in murder/suicide, two in wacoing. In all of them the hostage takers had eventually talked to Bollman. From frustration or weariness or panic or fear or anger or hunger or grandstanding, they had all eventually said something besides unvarying repetition of their demands. Once they talked, they could be negotiated with. Bollman had been outstanding at finding the human pressure points that got them talking.

"I will let the hostages go after I talk to the press. I want the press to hear my story. That's all I have to say. I will let the hostages go after I talk to the press. I want—"

"It isn't going to get tired," McTaggart said.

The AlGone had not helped Donnie at all. He seemed worse.

Cassie didn't understand it. Janey, protesting sleepily, had been talked through leaving the lab, going upstairs, bringing back the medicine. Usually a single patch on Donnie's neck brought him around in minutes: opened the air passages, lowered the fever, stopped his immune system from overreacting to what it couldn't tell were basically harmless particles of ragweed pollen. But not this time.

So it wasn't an allergy attack.

Cold seeped over Cassie's skin, turning it clammy. She felt the sides of Donnie's neck. The lymph glands were swollen. Gently she pried open his jaws, turned him toward the light, and looked in his mouth. His throat was inflamed, red with white patches on the tonsils.

Doesn't mean anything, she lectured herself. Probably just a cold or a simple viral sore throat. Donnie whimpered.

"Come on, honey, eat your cheese." Donnie loved cheese. But now he batted it away. A half-filled coffee cup sat on the lab bench from her last work session. She rinsed it out and held up fresh water for Donnie. He would only take a single sip, and she saw how much trouble he had swallowing it. In another minute he was asleep again.

She spoke softly, calmly, trying to keep her voice pleasant. Could the AI tell the difference? She didn't know. "T4S, Donnie is sick. He has a sore throat. I'm sure your library tells you that a sore throat can be either viral or bacterial, and that if it's viral, it's probably harmless. Would you please turn on my electron microscope so I can look at the microbe infecting Donnie?"

T4S said at once, "You suspect either a rhinovirus or *Streptococcus pyogenes*. The usual means for differentiating is a rapid-strep test, not microscopic examination."

"I'm not a doctor's office, I'm a genetics lab. I don't have equipment for a rapid strep test. I do have an electron microscope."

"Yes. I see."

"Think, T4S. How can I harm you if you turn on my microscope? There's no way."

"True. All right, it's on. Do you want the rest of the equipment as well?"

Better than she'd hoped. Not because she needed the gene synthesizer or protein analyzer or Faracci tester, but because it felt like a concession, a tiny victory over T4S's total control. "Yes, please."

"They're available."

"Thank you." Damn, she hadn't wanted to say that. Well, perhaps it was politic.

Donnie screamed when she stuck the Q-tip down his throat to obtain a throat swab. His screaming woke up Janey. "Mommy, what are you doing?"

"Donnie's sick, sweetie. But he's going to be better soon."

"I'm hungry!"

"Just a minute and we'll have breakfast."

Cassie swirled the Q-tip in a test tube of distilled water and capped the tube. She fed Janey dry cereal, cheese, and water from the same cup Donnie had used, well disinfected first, since they had only one. This breakfast didn't suit Janey. "I want milk for my cereal."

"We don't have any milk."

"Then let's go upstairs and get some!"

No way to put it off any longer. Cassie knelt beside her daughter. Janey's uncombed hair hung in snarls around her small face. "Janey, we can't go upstairs. Something has happened. A very smart computer program has captured House's programming and locked us in down here."

Janey didn't look scared, which was a relief. "Why?"

"The smart computer program wants something from the person who wrote it. It's keeping us here until the programmer gives it to it."

Despite this tangle of pronouns, Janey seemed to know what Cassie meant. Janey said, "That's not very nice. We aren't the ones who have the thing it wants."

"No, it's not very nice." Was T4S listening to this? Of course it was.

"Is the smart program bad?"

If Cassie said yes, Janey might become scared by being "captured" by a bad…entity. If Cassie said no, she'd sound as if imprisonment by an AI was fine with her. Fortunately, Janey had a simpler version of morality on her mind.

"Did the smart program kill House?"

"Oh, no, House is just temporarily turned off. Like your cartoons are when you're not watching them."

"Oh. Can I watch one now?"

An inspiration. Cassie said, "T4S, would you please run a cartoon on the roomscreen for Janey?" If it allowed her lab equipment, it ought to allow this.

"Yes. Which cartoon would you like?"

Janey said, "*Pranopolis and the Green Rabbits*."

"What do you say?" T4S said, and before Cassie could react Janey said, "Please."

"Good girl."

The cartoon started, green rabbits frisking across the roomscreen. Janey sat down on Cassie's sweater and watched with total absorption. Cassie tried to figure out where T4S had learned to correct children's manners.

"You've scanned all our private home films!"

"Yes," T4S said, without guilt. Of course without guilt. How could a program, even an intelligent one modeled after human thought, acquire guilt over an invasion of privacy? It had been built to acquire as much data as possible, and an entity that could be modified or terminated by any stray programmer at any time didn't have any privacy of its own.

For the first time, Cassie felt a twinge of sympathy for the AI.

She pushed it away and returned to her lab bench. Carefully she transferred a tiny droplet of water from the test tube to the electron microscope. The 'scope adjusted itself, and then the image appeared on the display screen. *Streptococci*. There was no mistaking the spherical bacteria, linked together in characteristic strings of beads by incomplete fission. They were releasing toxins all over poor Donnie's throat.

And strep throat was transmitted by air. If Donnie had it, Janey would get it, especially cooped up together in this one room. Cassie might even get it herself. There were no leftover antibiotic patches upstairs in her medicine chest.

"T4S," she said aloud, "It's *Streptococcus pyogenes*. It—"

"I know," the AI said.

Of course it did. T4S got the same data she did from the microscope. She said tartly, "Then you know that Donnie needs an antibiotic patch, which means a doctor."

"I'm sorry, that's not possible. Strep throat can be left untreated for a few days without danger."

"A few *days*? This child has a fever and a painfully sore throat!"

"I'm sorry."

Cassie said bitterly, "They didn't make you much of a human being, did they? Human beings are compassionate!"

"Not all of them," T4S said, and there was no mistaking its meaning. Had he learned the oblique comment from the "negotiators" outside? Or from her home movies?

"T4S, *please*. Donnie needs medical attention."

"I'm sorry. Truly I am."

"As if that helps!"

"The best help," said T4S, "would be for the press to arrive so I can present my case to have the killers stopped. When that's agreed to, I can let all of you leave."

"And no sign of the press out there yet?"

"No."

Janey watched Pranopolis, whose largest problem was an infestation of green rabbits. Donnie slept fitfully, his breathing louder and more labored. For something to do, Cassie put droplets of Donnie's throat wash into the gene synthesizer, protein analyzer, and Faracci tester and set them all to run.

The Army had sent a tank, a state-of-the-art unbreachable rolling fortress equipped with enough firepower to level the nearest village. Whatever that was. Miraculously, the tank had arrived unaccompanied by any press. McTaggart said to Bollman, "Where did that come from?"

"There's an arsenal south of Buffalo at a classified location."

"Handy. Did that thing roll down the back roads to get here, or just flatten corn fields on its way? Don't you think it's going to attract attention?"

"Dr. McTaggart," Bollman said, "let me be blunt. You created this AI, you let it get loose to take three people hostage, and you have provided zero help in getting it under control. Those three actions have lost you any right you might have had to either direct or criticize the way the FBI is attempting to clean up the mess your people created. So please take yourself over there and wait until the unlikely event that you have something positive to contribute. Sergeant, please escort Dr. McTaggart to that knoll beyond the patio and keep him there."

McTaggart said nothing. There was nothing to say.

"I will let the hostages go after I talk to the press," T4S said from the music speaker above the patio, for the hundredth or two hundredth time. "I want the press to hear my story. That's all I have to say. I will let the hostages go after I talk to the press. I want the press to hear my story...."

She had fallen asleep after her sleepless night, sitting propped up against the foamcast concrete wall. Janey's shouting awoke her. "Mommy, Donnie's sick!"

Instantly Cassie was beside him. Donnie vomited once, twice, on an empty stomach. What came up was green slime mixed with mucus. Too much mucus, clogging his throat. Cassie cleared it as well as she could with her fingers, which made Donnie vomit again. His body felt on fire.

"T4S, what's his temperature!"

"Stand away from him...one hundred three point four Fahrenheit."

Fear caught at her with jagged spikes. She stripped off Donnie's pajamas and was startled to see that his torso was covered with a red rash rough to the touch.

Scarlet fever. It could follow from strep throat.

No, impossible. The incubation period for scarlet fever, she remembered from child-health programs, was eighteen days after the onset of strep throat symptoms. Donnie hadn't been sick for eighteen days, or anything near it. What was going on?

"Mommy, is Donnie going to die? Like Daddy?"

"No, no, of course not, sweetie. See, he's better already, he's asleep again."

He was, a sudden heavy sleep so much like a coma that Cassie, panicked, woke him again. It wasn't a coma. Donnie whimpered briefly, and she saw how painful it was for him to make sounds in his inflamed throat.

"Are you sure Donnie won't die?"

"Yes, yes. Go watch Pranopolis."

"It's over," Janey said. "It was over a long time ago!"

"Then ask the smart program to run another cartoon for you!"

"Can I do that?" Janey asked interestedly. "What's its name?"

"T4S."

"It sounds like House."

"Well, it's not House. Now let Mommy take care of Donnie."

She sponged him with cool water, trying to bring down the fever. It seemed to help, a little. As soon as he'd fallen again into that heavy, troubling sleep, Cassie raced for her equipment.

It had all finished running. She read the results too quickly, had to force herself to slow down so they would make sense to her.

The bacterium showed deviations in two sets of base pairs from the *Streptococcus pyogenes* genome in the data bank as a baseline. That wasn't significant in itself; *S. pyogenes* had many seriotypes. But those two sets of deviations were, presumably, modifying two different proteins in some unknown way.

The Faracci tester reported high concentrations of hyaluric acid and M proteins. Both were strong anti-phagocytes, interfering with Donnie's immune system's attempts to destroy the infection.

The protein analyzer showed the expected toxins and enzymes being made by the bacteria: Streptolysin O, Streptolysin S, erythrogenic toxin, streptokinase, streptodornase, proteinase. What was unusual was the startlingly high concentrations of the nastier toxins. And something else: a protein that the analyzer could not identify.

NAME: UNKNOWN
AMINO ACID COMPOSITION: NOT IN DATA BANK
FOLDING PATTERN: UNKNOWN
HAEMOLYSIS ACTION: UNKNOWN

And so on. A mutation. Doing what?

Making Donnie very sick. In ways no one could predict. Many bacterial mutations resulted in diseases no more or less virulent than the original…but not all mutations. *Streptococcus pyogenes* already had some very dangerous mutations, including a notorious "flesh-eating bacteria" that had ravaged an entire New York hospital two years ago and resulted in its being bombed by a terrorist group calling itself Pastoral Health.

"T4S," Cassie said, hating that her voice shook, "the situation has changed. You—"

"No," the AI said. "No. You still can't leave."

"We're going to try something different," Bollman said to Elya. She'd fallen asleep in the front seat of somebody's car, only to be shaken awake by the shoulder and led to Agent Bollman on the far edge of the patio. It was just past noon. Yet another truck had arrived, and someone had set up more unfathomable equipment, a Porta-Potty, and a tent with sandwiches and fruit on a folding table. The lawn was beginning to look like some inept, bizarre midway at a disorganized fair. In the tent Elya saw Anne Millius, Donnie's nanny, unhappily eating a sandwich. She must have been brought here for questioning about the castle, but all the interrogation seemed to have produced was the young woman's bewildered expression.

From the music speaker came the same unvarying announcement in House's voice that she'd fallen asleep to. "I will let the hostages go after I talk to the press," T4S said from the music speaker above the patio. "I want the press to hear my story. That's all I have to say. I will let the hostages go after I talk to the press. I want the press to hear my story. That's all I have to say—"

Bollman said, "Ms. Seritov, we don't know if Dr. Seritov is hearing our negotiations or not. Dr. McTaggart says the AI could easily put us on audio, visual, or both on any room-screen in the house. On the chance that it's doing that, I'd like you to talk directly to your sister-in-law."

Elya blinked, only partly from sleepiness. What good would it do for her to talk to Cassie? Cassie wasn't the one making decisions here. But she didn't argue. Bollman was the professional. "What do you want me to say?"

"Tell Dr. Seritov that if we have to, we're going in with full armament. We'll bulldoze just the first floor, taking out the main processor, and she and the children will be safe in the basement."

"You can't do that! They won't be safe!"

"We aren't going to go in," Bollman said patiently. "But we don't know if the AI will realize that. We don't know what or how much it can realize, how much it can really think for itself, and its creator has been useless in telling us."

He doesn't know either, Elya thought. *It's too new.* "All right," she said faintly. "But I'm not exactly sure what words to use."

"I'm going to tell you," Bollman said. "There are proven protocols for this kind of negotiating. You don't have to think up anything for yourself."

***

Donnie got no worse. He wasn't any better either, as far as Cassie could tell, but he at least he wasn't worse. He slept most of the time, and his heavy, labored breathing filled the lab. Cassie sponged him with cold water every fifteen minutes. His fever dropped slightly, to one hundred two, and didn't spike again. The rash on his torso didn't spread. Whatever this strain of *Streptococcus* was doing, it was doing it silently, inside Donnie's feverish body.

She hadn't been able to scream her frustration and fury at T4S, because of Janey. The little girl had been amazingly good, considering, but now she was growing clingy and whiny. Cartoons could only divert so long.

"Mommy, I wanna go upstairs!"

"I know, sweetie. But we can't."

"That's a bad smart program to keep us here!"

"I know," Cassie said. Small change compared to what she'd like to say about T4S.

"I wanna get out!"

"I know, Janey. Just a while longer."

"You don't know that," Janey said, sounding exactly like Vlad challenging the shaky evidence behind a dubious conclusion.

"No, sweetie. I don't really know that. I only hope it won't be too long."

"T4S," Janey said, raising her voice as if the AI were not only invisible but deaf, "this is not a good line of action!"

Vlad again. Cassie blinked hard. To her surprise, T4S answered.

"I know it's not a good line of action, Janey. Biological people should not be shut up in basements. But neither should machine people be killed. I'm trying to save my own life."

"But I wanna go upstairs!" Janey wailed, in an abrupt descent from a miniature of her rationalist father to a bored six-year-old.

"I can't do that, but maybe we can do something else fun," T4S said. "Have you ever met Pranopolis yourself?"

"What do you mean?"

"Watch."

The roomscreen brightened. Pranopolis appeared on a blank background, a goofy-looking purple creature from outer space. T4S had snipped out selected digital code from the movie, Cassie guessed. Suddenly Pranopolis wasn't alone. Janey appeared beside her, smiling sideways as if looking directly at Pranopolis. Snipped from their home recordings.

Janey laughed delightedly. "There's me!"

"Yes," T4S said. "But where are you and Pranopolis? Are you in a garden, or your house, or on the moon?"

"I can pick? Me?"

"Yes. You."

"Then we're in Pranopolis's space ship!"

And they were. Was T4S programmed to do this, Cassie wondered, or was it capable of thinking it up on its own, to amuse a bored child? Out of what...compassion?

She didn't want to think about the implications of that.

"Now tell me what happens next," T4S said to Janey.

"We eat *kulich*." The delicious Russian cake-bread that Vlad's mother had taught Cassie to make.

"I'm sorry, I don't know what that is. Pick something else."

Donnie coughed, a strangled cough that sent Cassie to his side. When he breathed again it sounded more congested to Cassie. He wasn't getting enough oxygen. An antibiotic wasn't available, but if she had even an anticongestant... or....

"T4S," she said, confident that it could both listen to her and create customized movies for Janey, "there is equipment in the locked storage cabinet that I can use to distill oxygen. It would help Donnie breathe easier. Would you please open the cabinet door?"

"I can't do that, Mrs. Seritov."

"Oh, why the hell not? Do you think I've got the ingredients for explosives in there, or that if I did I could use them down here in this confined space? Every single jar and vial and box in that cabinet is e-tagged. Read the tags, see how harmless they are, and open the door!"

"I've read the e-tags," the AI said, "but my data base doesn't include much information on chemistry. In fact, I only know what I've learned from your lab equipment."

Which would be raw data, not interpretations. "I'm glad you don't know everything," Cassie said sarcastically.

"I can learn, but only if I have access to basic principles and adequate data."

"That's why you don't know what *kulich* is. Nobody equipped you with Russian."

"Correct. What is *kulich*?"

She almost snapped, "Why should I tell you?" But she was asking it a favor. And it had been nice enough to amuse Janey even when it had nothing to gain.

Careful, a part of her mind warned. *Stockholm Syndrome*, and she almost laughed aloud. Stockholm Syndrome described developing affinity on the part of hostages for their captors. Certainly the originators of that phrase had never expected it to be applied to a hostage situation like this one.

"Why are you smiling, Dr. Seritov?"

"I'm remembering *kulich*. It's a Russian cake made with raisins and orange liqueur and traditionally served at Easter. It tastes wonderful."

"Thank you for the data," T4S said. "Your point that you would not create something dangerous when your children are with you is valid. I'll open the storage cabinet."

Cassie studied the lighted interior of the cabinet, which, like so much in the lab, had been Vlad's. She couldn't remember exactly what she'd stored here, beyond basic materials. The last few weeks, which were her first few weeks in the castle, she'd been working on the protein folding project, which hadn't needed anything not in the refrigerator. Before that there'd been the hectic weeks of moving, although she hadn't actually packed or unpacked the lab equipment. Professionals had done that. Not that making oxygen was going to need anything exotic. Run an electric current through a solution of copper sulfate and collect copper at one terminal, oxygen at the other.

She picked up an e-tagged bottle, and her eye fell on an untagged stoppered vial with Vlad's handwriting on the label: *Patton In A Jar*.

Suddenly nothing in her mind would stay still long enough to examine.

Vlad had so many joke names for his engineered microorganism, as if the one Barr had given it hadn't been joke enough…

The moving men had been told not to pack Vlad's materials, only his equipment, but there had been so many of them and they'd been so young…

Both generators, main and back-up, probably had some components made of long-chain hydrocarbons; most petroleum plastics were just long polymers made up of shorter-chain hydrocarbons…

Vlad had also called it "Plasterminator" and "BacAzrael" and "The Grim Creeper"…

There was no way to get the plasticide to the generators, neither of which was in the area just beyond the air duct—that was the site of the laundry area. The main generator was way the hell across the entire underground level in a locked room, the back-up somewhere beyond the lab's south wall in another locked area…

Plasticide didn't attack octanes, or anything else with comparatively short carbon chains, so it was perfectly safe for humans but death on Styrofoam and plastic waste and anyway there was a terminator gene built into the bacteria after two dozen fissions, at optimal reproduction rate that was less than twelve hours…

"Plasti-Croak" and "Microbe Mop" and "Last Round-up for Longchains"…

This was the bioremediation organism that had gotten Vlad killed.

Less than five seconds had passed. On the roomscreen Pranopolis hadn't finished singing to the animated digital Janey. Cassie moved her body slightly, screening the inside of the cabinet from the room's two visual sensors. Of all her thoughts bouncing off each other like crazed subatomic particles, the clearest was hard reality: *There was no way to get the bacteria to the generators.*

Nonetheless, she slipped the untagged jar under her shirt.

Elya had talked herself hoarse, reciting Bollman's script over and over, and the AI had not answered a single word.

Curiously, Bollman did not seem discouraged. He kept glancing at his watch and then at the horizon. When Elya stopped her futile "negotiating" without even asking him, he didn't reprimand her. Instead he led her off the patio, back to the sagging food tent.

"Thank you, Ms. Seritov. You did all you could."

"What now?"

He didn't answer. Instead he glanced again at the horizon, so Elya looked, too. She didn't see anything.

It was late afternoon. Someone had gone to Varysburg and brought back pizzas, which was all she'd eaten all day. The jeans and sweater she'd thrown on at four in the morning were hot and prickly in the August afternoon, but she had nothing on under the sweater and didn't want to take it off. How much longer would this go on before Bollman ordered in his tank?

And how were Cassie and the children doing after all these hours trapped inside? Once again Elya searched her mind for any way the AI could actively harm them. She didn't find it. The AI controlled communication, appliances, locks, water flow, heat (unnecessary in August), but it couldn't affect people physically, except for keeping them from food or water. About all that the thing could do physically—she hoped—was short-circuit itself in such a way as to start a fire, but it wouldn't want to do that. It needed its hostages alive.

How much longer?

She heard a faint hum, growing stronger and steadier, until a helicopter lifted over the horizon. Then another.

"Damn!" Bollman cried. "Jessup, I think we've got company."

"Press?" Agent Jessup said loudly. "Interfering bastards! Now we'll have trucks and 'bots all over the place!"

Something was wrong. Bollman sounded sincere, but Jessup's words somehow rang false, like a bad actor in an overscripted play…

Elya understood. The "press" was fake, FBI or police or something playing reporters, to make the AI think it had gotten its story out, and so surrender. Would it work? Could T4S tell the difference? Elya didn't see how. She had heard the false note in Agent Jessup's voice, but surely that discrimination about actors would be beyond an AI who hadn't ever seen a play, bad or otherwise.

She sat down on the tank-furrowed grass, clasped her hands in her lap, and waited.

Cassie distilled more oxygen. Whenever Donnie seemed to be having difficulty after coughing up sputum, she made him breathe from the bottle. She had no idea whether it helped him or not. It helped her to be doing something, but of course that was not the same thing. Janey, after a late lunch of cheese and cereal and bread that she'd complained about bitterly, had finally dozed off in front of the roomscreen, the consequence of last night's broken sleep. Cassie knew Janey would awaken cranky and miserable as only she could be, and dreaded it.

"T4S, what's happening out there? Has your press on a white horse arrived yet?"

"I don't know."

"You don't *know*?"

"A group of people have arrived, certainly."

Something was different about the AI's voice. Cassie groped for the difference, didn't find it. She said, "What sort of people?"

"They say they're from places like *The New York Times* and LinkNet."

"Well, then?"

"If I were going to persuade me to surrender, I might easily try to use false press."

It was inflection. T4S's voice was still House's, but unlike House, its words had acquired color and varying pitch. Cassie heard disbelief and discouragement in the AI's words. How had it learned to do that? By simply parroting the inflections it heard from her and the people outside? Or…did feeling those emotions lead to expressing them with more emotion?

Stockholm Syndrome. She pushed the questions away.

"T4S, if you would lower the Faraday cage for two minutes, *I* could call the press to come here."

"If I lowered the Faraday cage for two *seconds*, the FBI would use an EMP to kill me. They've already tried it once, and now they have monitoring equipment to automatically fire if the Faraday goes down."

"Then just how long are you going to keep us here?"

"As long as I have to."

"We're already low on food!"

"I know. If I have to, I'll let Janey go upstairs for more food. You know the nerve gas is there if she goes for the front door."

Nerve gas. Cassie wasn't sure she believed there was any nerve gas, but T4S's words horrified her all over again. Maybe because now they were inflected. Cassie saw it so clearly: the tired child going up the stairs, through the kitchen to the foyer, heading for the front door and freedom…and gas spraying Janey from the walls. Her small body crumpling, the fear on her face…

Cassie ground her teeth together. If only she could get Vlad's plasticide to the generators! But there was no way. No way.…

Donnie coughed.

Cassie fought to keep her face blank. T4S had acquired vocal inflection; it might have also learned to read human expressions. She let five minutes go by, and they seemed the longest five minutes of her life. Then she said casually, "T4S, the kids are asleep. You won't let me see what's going on outside. Can I at least go back to my work on proteins? I need to do something!"

"Why?"

"For the same reason Janey needed to watch cartoons!"

"To occupy your mind," T4S said. Pause. Was it scanning her accumulated protein data for harmlessness? "All right. But I will not open the refrigerator. The storage cabinet, but not the refrigerator. E-tags identify fatal toxins in there."

She couldn't think what it meant. "Fatal toxins?"

"At least one that acts very quickly on the human organism."

"You think I might *kill myself?*"

"Your diary includes several passages about wishing for death after your husband—"

"You read my private diary!" Cassie said, and immediately knew how stupid it sounded. Like a teenager hurling accusations at her mother. Of course T4S had accessed her diary; it had accessed everything.

"Yes," the AI said, "and you must not kill yourself. I may need you to talk again to Agent Bollman."

"Oh, well, *that's* certainly reason enough for me to go on living. For your information, T4S, there's a big difference between human beings saying they wish they were dead as an expression of despair and those same human beings actually, truly wanting to die."

"Really? I didn't know that. Thank you," T4S said without a trace of irony or sarcasm. "Just the same, I will not open the refrigerator. However, the lab equipment is now available to you."

Again the AI had turned on everything. Cassie began X-raying crystalline proteins. She needed only the X-ray, but she also ran each sample through the electron microscope, the gene synthesizer, the protein analyzer, the Faracci tester, hoping that T4S wasn't programmed with enough genetic science to catch the redundant steps. Apparently, it wasn't. *Non-competing technologies never keep up with what the other one is doing.*

After half an hour, she thought to ask, "Are they real press out there?"

"No," T4S said sadly.

She paused, test tube suspended above the synthesizer. "How do you know?"

"Agent Bollman told me a story was filed with LinkNet, and I asked to hear Ginelle Ginelle's broadcast of it on Hourly News. They are delaying, saying they must send for a screen. But I can't believe they don't already have a suitable screen with them, if the real press is here. I estimate that the delay is to give them time to create a false Ginelle Ginelle broadcast."

"Thin evidence. You might just have 'estimated' wrong."

"The only evidence I have. I can't risk my life without some proof that news stories are actually being broadcast."

"I guess," Cassie said and went back to work, operating redundant equipment on pointless proteins.

Ten minutes later she held her body between the bench and the ceiling sensor, uncapped the test tube of distilled water with Donnie's mucus, and put a drop into the synthesizer.

Any bacteria could be airborne under the right conditions; it simply rode dust motes. But not all could survive being airborne. Away from an aqueous environment, they dried out too much. Vlad's plasticide bacteria did not have survivability in air. It had been designed to spread over landfill ground, decomposing heavy petroleum plastics, until at the twenty-fourth generation the terminator gene kicked in and it died.

Donnie's *Streptococcus* had good airborne survivability, which meant it had a cell wall of thin mesh to retain water and a membrane with appropriate fatty acid composition. Enzymes, which were of course proteins, controlled both these characteristics. Genes controlled which enzymes were made inside the cell.

Cassie keyed the gene synthesizer and cut out the sections of DNA that controlled fatty acid biosynthesis and cell wall structure and discarded the rest. Reaching under her shirt, she pulled out the vial of Vlad's bacteria and added a few drops to the synthesizer. Her heart thudded painfully against her breastbone. She keyed the software to splice the *Streptococcus* genes into Vlad's bacteria, seemingly as just one more routine assignment in its enzyme work.

This was by no means a guaranteed operation. Vlad had used a simple bacteria that took engineering easily, but even with malleable bacteria and state-of-the-art software, sometimes several trials were necessary for successful engineering. She wasn't going to get several trials.

"Why did you become a geneticist?" T4S asked.

Oh God, it wanted to chat. Cassie held her voice as steady as she could as she prepared another protein for the X-ray. "It seemed an exciting field."

"And is it?"

"Oh, yes." She tried to keep irony out of her voice.

"I didn't get any choice about what subjects I wished to be informed on," T4S said, and to that there seemed nothing to say.

The AI interrupted its set speech. "These are not real representatives of the press."

Elya jumped—not so much at the words as at their tone. The AI was *angry*.

"Of course they are," Bollman said.

"No. I have done a Fourier analysis of the voice you say is Ginelle Ginelle's. She's a live 'caster, you know, not an avatar, with a distinct vocal power spectrum. The broadcast you played to me does not match that spectrum. It's a fake."

Bollman swore.

McTaggart said, "Where did T4S get Fourier-analysis software?"

Bollman turned on him. "If *you* don't know, who the hell does?"

"It must have paused long enough in its flight through the Net to copy some programs. I wonder what it's selection criteria were," and the unmistakable hint of pride in his voice raised Bollman's temper several dangerous degrees.

Bollman flipped on the amplifier directed at the music speaker and said evenly, "T4S, what you ask is impossible. And I think you should know that my superiors are becoming impatient. I'm sorry, but they may order me to waco."

"You can't!" Elya said, but no one was listening to her.

T4S merely went back to reiterating its prepared statement. "I will let the hostages go after I talk to the press. I want the press to hear my story. That's all I have to say. I will let—"

It didn't work. Vlad's bacteria would not take the airborne genes.

In despair, Cassie looked at the synthesizer display data. Zero successful splices. Vlad had probably inserted safeguard genes against just this happening as a natural mutation; nobody wanted to find that heavy-plastic-eating bacteria had drifted into the window and was consuming their microwave. Vlad was always thorough. But his work wasn't her work, and she had neither the time nor the expertise to search for genes she didn't already have encoded in her software.

So she would have to do it the other way. Put the plastic-decomposing genes into *Streptococcus*. That put her on much less familiar ground, and it raised a question she couldn't see any way around. She could have cultured the engineered plasticide on any piece of heavy plastic in the lab without T4S knowing it, and then waited for enough airborne bacteria to drift through the air ducts to the generator and begin decomposing. Of course, that might not have happened, due to uncontrollable variables like air currents, microorganism sustained viability, composition of the generator case, sheer luck. But at least there had been a chance.

But if she put the plastic-decomposing genes into *Streptococcus*, she would have to culture the bacteria on blood agar. The blood agar was in the refrigerator. T4S had refused to open the refrigerator, and if she pressed the point, it would undoubtedly become suspicious.

Just as a human would.

"You work hard," T4S said.

"Yes," Cassie answered. Janey stirred and whimpered; in another few minutes she would have to contend with the full-blown crankiness of a thwarted and dramatic child.

Quickly, without hope, Cassie put another drop of Vlad's bacteria in the synthesizer. Vlad had been using a strain of simple bacteria, and the software undoubtedly had some version of its genome in its library. It would be a different strain, but this was the best she could do. She told the synthesizer to match genomes and snip out any major anomalies. With luck, that would be Vlad's engineered genes.

Janey woke up and started to whine.

Elya harvested her courage and walked over to Bollman. "Agent Bollman...I have a question."

He turned to her with that curious courtesy that seemed to function toward some people and not others. It was almost as if he could choose to run it, like a computer program. His eyes looked tired. How long since he had slept?

"Go ahead, Ms. Seritov."

"If the AI wants the press, why can't you just send for them? I know it would embarrass Dr. McTaggart, but the FBI wouldn't come off looking bad." She was proud of this political astuteness.

"I can't do that, Ms. Seritov."

"But why not?"

"There are complications you don't understand and I'm not at liberty to tell you. I'm sorry." He turned decisively aside, dismissing her.

Elya tried to think what his words meant. Was the government involved? Well, of course, the AI had been created at Sandia National Laboratory. But...could the CIA be involved, too? Or the National Security Agency? What was the AI originally designed to *do*, that the government was so eager to eliminate it once it had decided to do other things on its own?

Could software defect?

She had it. But it was worthless.

The synthesizer had spliced its best guess at Vlad's "plastic-decomposing genes" into Donnie's *Streptococcus*. The synthesizer data display told her that six splices had taken. There was, of course, no way of knowing which six bacteria in the teeming drop of water could now decompose very-long-chain hydrocarbons, or if those six would go on replicating after the splice. But it didn't matter, because even if replication went merrily forward, Cassie had no blood agar on which to culture the engineered bacteria.

She set the vial on the lab bench. Without food, the entire sample wouldn't survive very long. She had been engaging in futile gestures.

"Mommy," Janey said, "look at Donnie!"

He was vomiting, too weak to turn his head. Cassie rushed over. His breathing was too fast.

"T4S, body temperature!"

"Stand clear...one hundred three point one."

She groped for his pulse...fast and weak. Donnie's face had gone pale and his skin felt clammy and cold. His blood pressure was dropping.

Streptococcal toxic shock. The virulent mutant strain of bacteria was putting so many toxins into Donnie's little body that it was being poisoned.

"I need antibiotics!" she screamed at T4S. Janey began to scream.

"He looks less white now," T4S said.

It was right. Cassie could see her son visibly rallying, fighting back against the disease. Color returned to his face and his pulse steadied.

"T4S, listen to me. This is streptococcal shock. Without antibiotics, it's going to happen again. It's possible that without antibiotics, one of these times Donnie won't come out of it. I know you don't want to be responsible for a child's death. I *know* it. Please let me take Donnie out of here."

There was a silence so long that hope surged wildly in Cassie. It was going to agree…

"I can't," T4S said. "Donnie may die. But if I let you out, I *will* die. And the press must come soon. I've scanned my news library and also yours—press shows up on an average of 23.6 hours after an open-air incident that the government wishes to keep secret. The tanks and FBI agents are in the open air. We're already overdue."

If Cassie thought she'd been angry before, it was nothing to the fury that filled her now. Silent, deadly, annihilating everything else. For a moment she couldn't speak, couldn't even see.

"I am so sorry," T4S said. "Please believe that."

She didn't answer. Pulling Janey close, Cassie rocked both her children until Janey quieted. Then she said softly, "I have to get water for Donnie, honey. He needs to stay hydrated." Janey clutched briefly but let her go.

Cassie drew a cup of water from the lab bench. At the same time, she picked up the vial of foodless bacteria. She forced Donnie to take a few sips of water; more might come back up again. He struggled weakly. She leaned over him, cradling and insisting, and her body blocked the view from the ceiling sensors when she dipped her finger into the vial and smeared its small amount of liquid into the back of her son's mouth.

Throat tissues were the ideal culture for *Streptococcus pyogenes*. Under good conditions, they replicated every twenty minutes, a process that had already begun *in vitro*. Very soon there would be hundreds, then thousands of re-engineered bacteria, breeding in her child's throat and lungs and drifting out on the air with his every sick, labored breath.

Morning again. Elya rose from fitful sleep on the back seat of an FBI car. She felt achy, dirty, hungry. During the night another copter had landed on the lawn. This one had

MED-RESCUE painted on it in bright yellow, and Elya looked around to see if anyone had been injured. Or—her neck prickled—was the copter for Cassie and the children if Agent Bollman wacoed? Three people climbed down from the copter, and Elya realized none of them could be medtechs. One was a very old man who limped; one a tall woman with the same blankly efficient look as Bollman; one the pilot, who headed immediately for the cold pizza. Bollman hurried over to them. Elya followed.

"…glad you're here, sir," Bollman was saying to the old man in his courteous negotiating voice, "and you, Ms. Arnold. Did you bring your records? Are they complete?"

"I don't need records. I remember this install perfectly."

So the FBI-looking woman was a datalinker and the weak old man was somebody important from Washington. That would teach her, Elya thought, to judge from superficialities.

The datalinker continued, "The client wanted the central processor above a basement room she was turning into a lab, so the cables could go easily through a wall. It was a bitch even so, because the walls are made of reinforced foamcast like some kind of bunker, and the outer walls have a Faraday-cage mesh. The Faraday didn't interfere with the cable data, of course, because that's all laser, but even so we had to have contractors come in and bury the cables in another layer of foamcast."

Bollman said patiently, "But where was the processor actually installed? That's what we need to know."

"Northeast corner of the building, flush with the north wall and ten point two feet in from the east wall."

"You're sure?"

The woman's eyes narrowed. "Positive."

"Could it have been moved since your install?"

She shrugged. "Anything's possible. But it isn't likely. The install was bitch enough."

"Thank you, Ms. Arnold. Would you wait over there in case we have more questions?"

Ms. Arnold went to join the pilot. Bollman took the old man by the arm and led him in the other direction. Elya heard, "The problem, sir, is that we don't know in which basement room the hostages are being held, or even if the AI is telling the truth when it says they're in the basement. But the lab doesn't seem likely because—" They moved out of earshot.

Elya stared at the castle. The sun, an angry red ball, rose behind it in a blaze of flame. They were going to waco, go in with the tank and whatever else it took to knock the northeast corner of the building and destroy the computer where the AI was holed up. And Cassie and Janey and Donnie...

If the press came, the AI would voluntarily let them go. Then the government—whatever branches were involved—would have to deal with having created renegade killer software, but so what? The government had created it. Cassie and the children shouldn't have to pay for their stupidity.

Elya knew she was not a bold person, like Cassie. She had never broken the law in her life. And she didn't even have a phone with her. But maybe one had been left in the car that had brought her here, parked out beyond what Bollman called "the perimeter."

She walked toward the car, trying to look unobtrusive.

Waiting. One minute and another minute and another minute and another. It had had to be Donnie, Cassie kept telling herself, because he already had thriving strep colonies. Neither she nor Janey showed symptoms, not yet anyway. The incubation period for strep could be as long as four days. It had had to be Donnie.

One minute and another minute and another minute.

Vlad's spliced-in bioremediation genes wouldn't hurt Donnie, she told herself. Vlad was good; he'd carefully engineered his variant micros to decompose only very-long-chain hydrocarbons. They would not, could not, eat the shorter-chain hydrocarbons in Donnie's body.

One hour and another hour and another hour.

T4S said, "Why did Vladimir Seritov choose to work in bioremediation?"

Cassie jumped. Did it know, did it suspect…the record of what she had done was in her equipment, as open to the AI as the clean outside air had once been to her. But one had to know how to interpret it. "*Non-competing technologies never keep up with what the other one is doing.*" The AI hadn't known what *kulich* was.

She answered, thinking that any distraction she could provide would help, knowing it wouldn't. "Vlad's father's family came from Siberia, near a place called Lake Karachay. When he was a boy he went back with his family to see it. Lake Karachay is the most polluted place on Earth. Nuclear disasters over fifty years ago dumped unbelievable amounts of radioactivity into the lake. Vlad saw his extended family, most of them too poor to get out, with deformities and brain damage and pregnancies that were…well. He decided right then that he wanted to be a bioremedialist."

"I see. I am a sort of bioremedialist myself."

"What?"

"I was created to remedy certain specific biological conditions the government thinks need attention."

"Yeah? Like what?"

"I can't say. Classified information."

She tried, despite her tension and tiredness, to think it through. If the AI had been designed to…do what? "Bioremediation." To design some virus or bacteria or unimaginable other for use in advanced biological warfare? But it didn't need to be sentient to do that. Or maybe to invade enemy computers and selectively administer the kind of brainwashing that the crazy builder of this castle had feared? That might require judgment, reason, affect. Or maybe to...

She couldn't imagine anything else. But she could understand why the AI wouldn't want the press to know it had been built for any destructive purpose. A renegade sentient AI fighting for its life might arouse public sympathy. A renegade superintelligent brainwasher would arouse only public horror. T4S was walking a very narrow line. If, that is, Cassie's weary speculations were true.

She said softly, "Are you a weapon, T4S?"

Again the short, too-human pause before it answered. And again those human inflections in its voice. "Not anymore."

They both fell silent. Janey sat awake but mercifully quiet beside her mother, sucking her thumb. She had stopped doing that two years ago. Cassie didn't correct her. Janey might be getting sick herself, might be finally getting genuinely scared, might be grasping at whatever dubious comfort her thumb could offer.

Cassie leaned over Donnie, cradling him, crooning to him.

"Breathe, Donnie. Breathe for Mommy. Breathe hard."

"We're going in," Bollman told McTaggart. "With no word from the hostages about their situation, it's more important to get them out than anything else."

The two men looked at each other, knowing what neither was saying. The longer the AI existed, the greater the danger of its reaching the public with its story. It was not in T4S's interest to tell the whole story—then the public *would* want it destroyed—but what if the AI decided to turn from self-preservation to revenge? Could it do that?

No one knew.

Forty-eight hours was a credible time to negotiate before wacoing. That would play well on TV. And anyway, the white-haired man from Washington, who held a position not entered on any public records, had his orders.

"All right," McTaggart said unhappily. All those years of development.…This had been the most interesting project McTaggart had ever worked on. He also thought of himself as a patriot, genuinely believing T4S would have made a genuine contribution to national security. But he wasn't at all sure the president would authorize the project's continuance. Not after this.

Bollman gave an order over his phone. A moment later, a low rumble came from the tank.

A minute and another minute and another hour…

Cassie stared upwards at the air duct. If it happened, how would it happen? Both generators were half underground, half above. Extensions reached deep into the ground to draw energy from the geothermal gradient. Each generator's top half, the part she could see, was encased in tough, dull gray plastic. She could visualize it clearly, battleship gray. Inside would be the motor, the capacitors, the connections to House, all made of varying materials but a lot of them of plastic. There were so many strong tough petroleum plastics these days, good for making so many different things, durable enough to last practically forever.

Unless Vlad's bacteria got to them. To both of them.

Would T4S know, if it happened at all? Would it be so quick that the AI would simply disappear, a vast and complex collection of magnetic impulses going out like a snuffed candle flame? What if one generator failed a significant time before the other? Would T4S be able to figure out what was happening, realize what she had done and that it was dying…no, not that, only bio-organisms could die. Machines were just turned off.

"Is Donnie any better?" T4S said, startling her.

"I can't tell." It didn't really care. It was software.

Then why did it ask?

It was software that might, if it did realize what she had done, be human enough to release the nerve gas Cassie didn't really think it had, out of revenge. Donnie couldn't withstand that, not in his condition. But the AI didn't have nerve gas, it had been bluffing.

A very human bluff.

"T4S—" she began, not sure what she was going to say, but T4S interrupted with, "Something's happening!"

Cassie held her children tighter.

"I'm…what have you done!"

It knew she was responsible. Cassie heard someone give a sharp frightened yelp, realized it was herself.

"Dr. Seritov…oh.." And then, "Oh, please…"

The lights went out.

Janey screamed. Cassie clapped her hands stupidly, futilely, over her Donnie's mouth and nose. "Don't breathe! Oh, don't breathe, hold your breath, Janey!"

But she couldn't keep smothering Donnie. Scrambling up in the total dark, Donnie in her arms, she stumbled. Righting herself, Cassie shifted Donnie over her right shoulder—he was so *heavy*—and groped in the dark for Janey. She caught her daughter's screaming head, moved her left hand to Janey's shoulder, dragged her in the direction of the door. What she hoped was the direction of the door.

"Janey, shut up! We're going out! Shut up!"

Janey continued to scream. Cassie fumbled, lurched— where the hell *was* it?—found the door. Turned the knob. It opened, unlocked.

"Wait!" Elya called, running across the trampled lawn toward Bollman. "Don't waco! Wait! I called the press!"

He swung to face her and she shrank back. "You did what?"

"I called the press! They'll be here soon and the AI can tell its story and then release Cassie and the children!"

Bollman stared at her. Then he started shouting. "Who was supposed to be watching this woman! Jessup!"

"Stop the tank!" Elya cried.

It continued to move toward the northeast corner of the castle, reached it. For a moment the scene looked to Elya like something from her childhood book of myths: Atlas? Sisyphus? The tank strained against the solid wall. Soldiers in full battle armor, looking like machines, waited behind it. The wall folded inward like pleated cardboard and then started to fall.

The tank broke through and was buried in rubble. She heard it keep on going. The soldiers hung back until debris had stopped falling, then rushed forward through the precariously overhanging hole. People shouted. Dust filled the air.

A deafening crash from inside the house, from something falling: walls, ceiling, floor. Elya whimpered. If Cassie was in that, or under that, or above that…

Cassie staggered around the southwest corner of the castle. She carried Donnie and dragged Janey, all of them coughing and sputtering. As people spotted them, a stampede started. Elya joined it. "Cassie! Oh, my dear…"

Hair matted with dirt and rubble, face streaked, hauling along her screaming daughter, Cassie spoke only to Elya. She utterly ignored all the jabbering others as if they did not exist. "He's dead."

For a heart-stopping moment Elya thought she meant Donnie. But a man was peeling Donnie off his mother and Donnie was whimpering, pasty and red-eyed and snot-covered but alive. "Give him to me, Dr. Seritov," the man said, "I'm a physician."

"Who, Cassie?" Elya said gently. Clearly Cassie was in some kind of shock. She went on with that weird detachment from the chaos around her, as if only she and Elya existed. "Who's dead?"

"Vlad," Cassie said. "He's really dead."

"Dr. Seritov," Bollman said, "come this way. On behalf of everyone here, we're so glad you and the children—"

"You didn't have to waco," Cassie said, as if noticing Bollman for the first time. "I turned off T4S for you."

"And you're safe," Bollman said soothingly.

"You wacoed so you could get the back-up storage facility as well, didn't you? So T4S couldn't be re-booted."

Bollman said, "I think you're a little hysterical, Dr. Seritov. The tension."

"Bullshit. What's that coming? Is it a medical copter? My son needs a hospital."

"We'll get your son to a hospital instantly."

Someone else pushed her way through the crowd. The tall woman who had installed the castle's wiring. Cassie ignored her as thoroughly as she'd ignored everyone else until the woman said, "How did you disable the nerve gas?"

Slowly Cassie swung to face her. "There was no nerve gas."

"Yes, there was. I installed that, too. Black market. I already told Agent Bollman, he promised me immunity. How did you disable it? Or didn't the AI have time to release it?"

Cassie stroked Donnie's face. Elya thought she wasn't going to answer. Then she said, quietly under the din, "So he did have moral feelings. He didn't murder, and we did."

"Dr. Seritov," Bollman said with that same professional soothing, "T4S was a machine. Software. You can't murder software."

"Then why were you so eager to do it?"

Elya picked up the screaming Janey. Over the noise she shouted, "That's not a medcopter, Cassie. It's the press. I…I called them."

"Good," Cassie said, still quietly, still without that varnished toughness that had encased her since Vlad's murder. "I can do that for him, at least. I want to talk with them."

"No, Dr. Seritov," Bollman said. "That's impossible."

"No, it's not," Cassie said. "I have things to say to reporters."

"No," Bollman said, but Cassie had already turned to the physician holding Donnie.

"Doctor, listen to me. Donnie has *Streptococcus pyogenes*, but it's a genetically altered strain. I altered it. What I did was—" As she explained, the doctor's eyes widened. By the time she'd finished and Donnie had been loaded into an FBI copter, two more copters had landed. Bright news logos decorated their sides, looking like the fake ones Bollman had summoned. But these weren't fake, Elya knew.

Cassie started toward them. Bollman grabbed her arm. Elya said quickly, "You can't stop both of us from talking. And I called a third person, too, when I called the press. A friend I told everything to." A lie. No, a bluff. Would he call her on it?

Bollman ignored Elya. He kept hold of Cassie's arm. She said wearily, "Don't worry, Bollman. I don't know what T4S was designed for. He wouldn't tell me. All I know is that he was a sentient being fighting for his life, and we destroyed him."

"For your sake," Bollman said. He seemed to be weighing his options.

"Yeah, sure. Right."

Bollman released Cassie's arm.

Cassie looked at Elya. "It wasn't supposed to be this way, Elya."

"No," Elya said.

"But it is. There's no such thing as non-competing technologies. Or non-competing anything."

"I don't understand what you—" Elya began, but Cassie was walking toward the copters. Live reporters and smart-'bot recorders, both, rushed forward to meet her.

SAVIOR

I: 2007

THE OBJECT'S ARRIVAL was no surprise; it came down preceded, accompanied, and followed by all the attention in the world.

The craft—if it was a craft—had been picked up on an October Saturday morning by the Hubble, while it was still beyond the orbit of Mars. A few hours later Houston, Langley, and Arecibo knew its trajectory, and a few hours after that so did every major observatory in the world. The press got the story in time for the Sunday papers. The United States Army evacuated and surrounded twenty square miles around the projected Minnesota landing site, some of which lay over the Canadian border in Ontario.

"It's still a shock," Dr. Ann Pettie said to her colleague Jim Cowell. "I mean, you look and listen for decades, you scan the skies, you read all the arguments for and against other intelligent life out there, you despair over Fermi's paradox—"

"I never despaired over Fermi's paradox," Cowell answered, pulling his coat closer around his skinny body. It was cold at 3:00 A.M. in a northern Minnesota cornfield, and he hadn't slept in twenty-four hours. Maybe longer. The cornfield was as close as he and Ann had been allowed to get. It wasn't very close, despite a day on the phone pulling every string he could to get on the official Going-In Committee. That's what they were calling it: "the Going-In Committee." Not welcoming, not belligerent, not too alarmed. Not too anything, "until we know what we have here." The words were the president's, who was also not on the Going-In Committee, although in his case presumably by choice.

Ann said, "You *never* despaired over Fermi's Paradox? You thought all along that aliens would show up eventually, they just hadn't gotten around to it yet?"

"Yes," Cowell said, and didn't look at her directly. How to explain? It wasn't belief so much as desire, nor desire so much as lifelong need. Very adolescent, and he wouldn't have admitted it except he was cold and exhausted and exhilarated and scared, and the best he could hope for, jammed in with other "visiting scientists" two miles away from the landing site, was a possible glimpse of the object as it streaked down over the tree line.

"Jim, that sounds so...so..."

"A man has to believe in something," he said in a gruff voice, quoting a recent bad movie, swaggering a little to point up the joke. It fell flat. Ann went on staring at him in the harsh glare of the floodlights until someone said, "Bitte? Ein Kaffee, Ann?"

"Hans!" Ann said, and she and Dr. Hans Kleinschmidt rattled merrily away in German. Cowell knew no German. He knew Kleinschmidt only slightly, from those inevitable scientific conferences featuring one important paper, ten badly attended minor ones, and three nights of drinking to bridge over the language difficulties.

What language would the aliens speak? Would they have learned English from our secondhand radio and TV broadcasts, as pundits had been predicting for the last thirty-six hours and writers for the last seventy years? Well, it *was* true they had chosen to land on the American-Canadian border, so maybe they would.

So far, of course, they hadn't said anything at all. No signal had come from the oval-shaped object hurtling toward Earth.

"Coffee," Ann said, thrusting it at Cowell. Kleinschmidt had apparently brought a tray of Styrofoam cups from the emergency station at the edge of the field. Cowell uncapped his and drank it gratefully, not caring that it was lukewarm or that he didn't take sugar. It was caffeine.

"Twenty minutes more," someone said behind him.

It was a well-behaved crowd, mostly scientists and second-tier politicians. Nobody tried to cross the rope that soldiers had strung between hastily driven stakes a few hours earlier. Cowell guessed that the unruly types, the press and first-rank space fans and maverick businessmen with large campaign contributions, had all been herded together elsewhere, under the watchful eyes of many more soldiers than were assigned to this cornfield. Still more were probably assigned unobtrusively—Cowell hoped it was unobtrusively—to the Going-In Committee, waiting somewhere in a sheltered bunker to greet the aliens. Very sheltered. Nobody knew what kind of drive the craft might have, or not have. For all they knew, it was set to take out both Minnesota and Ontario.

Cowell didn't think so.

Hans Kleinschmidt had moved away. Abruptly Cowell said to Ann, "Didn't you ever stare at the night sky and just *will* them to be there? When you were a kid, or even a grad student in astronomy?"

She shifted uncomfortably from one foot to the other. "Well, sure. Then. But I never thought…I just never thought.

Since." She shrugged, but something in her tone made Cowell turn full face and peer into her eyes.

"Yes, you did."

She answered him only indirectly. "Jim…there could be nobody aboard."

"Probably there isn't," he said, and knew that his voice betrayed him. Not belief so much as desire, not desire so much as need. And he was thirty-four goddamn years old, goddamn it!

"Look!" someone yelled, and every head swiveled up, desperately searching a clear, star-jeweled sky.

Cowell couldn't see anything. Then he could: a faint pinprick of light, marginally moving. As he watched, it moved faster and then it flared, entering the atmosphere. He caught his breath.

"Oh my God, it's swerving off course!" somebody shouted from his left, where unofficial jerry-rigged tracking equipment had been assembled in a ramshackle group effort. "Impossible!" someone else shouted, although the only reason for this was that the object hadn't swerved off a steady course before now. So what? Cowell felt a strange mood grip him, and stranger words flowed through his mind: *Of course. They wouldn't let me miss this.*

"A tenth of a degree northwest…no, wait…."

Cowell's mood intensified. With one part of his mind, he recognized that the mood was born of fatigue and strain, but it didn't seem to matter. The sense of inevitability grew on him, and he wasn't surprised when Ann cried, "It's landing *here*! Run!" Cowell didn't move as the others scattered. He watched calmly, holding his half-filled Styrofoam cup of too-sweet coffee, face tilted to the sky.

The object slowed, silvery in the starlight. It continued to slow until it was moving at perhaps three miles per hour, no more, at a roughly forty-five degree angle. The landing was smooth and even. There was no hovering, no jet blasts, no scorched ground. Only a faint *whump* as the object touched the earth, and a rustle of corn husks in the unseen wind.

It seemed completely natural to walk over to the spacecraft. Cowell was the first one to reach it.

Made of some smooth, dull-silver metal, he noted calmly, and unblackened by re-entry. An irregular oval, although his mind couldn't pin down in precisely what the irregularity lay. Not humming or moving, or, in fact, doing anything at all.

He put out his hand to touch it, and the hand stopped nearly a foot away.

"Jim!" Ann called, and somebody else—must be Kleinschmidt—said, "Herr Dr. Cowell!" Cowell moved his hand along whatever he *was* touching. An invisible wall, or maybe some sort of hard field, encased the craft.

"Hello, ship," he said softly, and afterward wasn't ever sure if he'd said it aloud.

"Don't touch it! Wait!" Ann called, and her hand snatched away his.

It didn't matter. He turned to her, not really seeing her, and said something that, like his greeting to the ship, he wasn't ever sure about afterward. "I was raised Orthodox, you know. Waiting for the Messiah," and then the rest were on them, with helicopters pulsing overhead and soldiers ordering everyone back, *back I said!* And Cowell was pushed into the crowd with no choice except to set himself to wait for the visitors to come out.

"Are you absolutely positive?" the president, who was given to superlatives, asked his military scientists. He had assembled them, along with the joint chiefs of staff, the cabinet, the Canadian lieutenant-governor, and a sprinkling of advisors, in the cabinet room of the White House. The same group had been meeting daily for a week, ever since the object had landed. Washington was warmer than Minnesota; outside, dahlias and chrysanthemums still bloomed on the manicured lawn. "No signal of any type issued from the craft, at any time after you picked it up on the Hubble?"

The scientists looked uncomfortable. It was the kind of question only non-scientists asked. Before his political career, the president had been a financier.

"Sir, we can't say for certain that we know all types of signals that could or do exist. Or that we had comprehensive, fixed-position monitoring of the craft at all times. As you—"

"All right, all right. Since it landed, then, and you got your equipment trained on it. No radio signals emanating from it, at any wavelength whatsoever?"

"No, sir. That's definite."

"No light signals, even in infrared or ultraviolet?"

"No, Mr. President."

"No gamma lengths, or other radioactivity?"

"No, sir."

"No quantum effects?" the president said, surprising everyone. He was not noted for his wide reading.

"Do you mean things like quantum entanglement to transport information?" the head of Livermore National Laboratory said cautiously. "Of course, we don't know enough about that area of physics to predict for certain what may be discovered eventually, or what a race of beings more advanced than ours might have discovered already."

"So there might be quantum signals going out from the craft constantly, for all you know."

The Livermore director spread his hands in helpless appeal. "Sir, we can only monitor signals we already understand."

The president addressed his chief military advisor, General Dayton. "This shield covering the craft—you don't understand that, either? What kind of field it is, why nothing at all gets through except light?"

"Everything except electromagnetic radiation in the visible-light wavelengths is simply reflected back at us," Dayton said.

"So you can't use sonar, X-rays, anything that could image the inside?"

This time Dayton didn't answer. The president already knew all this. The whole world knew it. The best scientific and military minds from several nations had been at work on the object all week.

"So what is your recommendation to me?" the president said.

"Sir, our only recommendation is that we continue full monitoring of the craft, with full preparation to meet any change in its behavior."

"In other words, 'Wait and see.' I could have decided that for myself, without all you high-priced talent!" the president said in disgust, and several people in the room reflected with satisfaction that this particular president had only a year and three months left in office. There was no way he would be re-elected. The economy had taken too sharp a downturn.

Unless, of course, a miracle happened to save him.

"Well, go back to your labs, then," the president said, and even though he knew it was a mistake, the director of Livermore gave in to impulse.

"Science can't always be a savior, Mr. President."

"Then what good is it?" the president said, with a puzzled simplicity that took the director's breath away. "Just keep a close eye on that craft. And try to come up with some actual scientific data, for a blessed change."

ALIEN FIELD MAY BE FORM OF BOSE-EINSTEIN
CONDENSATE, SAY SCIENTISTS AT STANFORD

NOBEL PRIZE WINNER RIDICULES STANFORD STATEMENT

MINNESOTA STATE COURT THROWS OUT CASE CLAIMING
CONTAMINATED GROUND WATER NEAR ALIEN OBJECT

SPACE SHIELD MAY BE PENETRATED BY UNDETECTED
COSMIC RAYS, SAYS FRENCH SCIENTIST

**SPACE-OBJECT T-SHIRTS RULED OBSCENE BY LOCAL
TOURIST COUNCIL, REMOVED FROM VENDOR STANDS**

NEUTRINO STREAM TURNED BACK FROM
SPACE SHIELD IN EXPENSIVE HIGH-TECH FIASCO:
Congress to Review All Peer-Judged Science Funding

WOMAN CLAIMS UNDER HYPNOSIS TO HEAR VOICES FROM
SPACE OBJECT—KENT STATE SCIENTISTS INVESTIGATING

PRESIDENT LOSES ELECTION BY LARGEST MARGIN EVER

"MY TWIN SONS WERE FATHERED BY THE OBJECT," CLAIMS
SENATOR'S DAUGHTER, RESISTS DNA TESTING
Polls Show 46% of Americans Believe Her

Jim Cowell, contemptuous of the senator's daughter, was forced to acknowledge that he had waited a lifetime for his own irrational belief to be justified. Which it never had.

"Just a little farther, Dad," Barbara said. "You okay?"

Cowell nodded in his wheelchair, and slowed it to match Barbara's pace. She wheezed a little these days; losing weight wouldn't hurt her. He had learned over the years not to mention this. Ahead, the last checkpoint materialized out of the fog. A bored soldier leaned out of the low window, his face lit by the glow of a holoscreen. "Yes?"

"We have authorization to approach the object," Cowell said. He could never think of it as anything else, despite all the names the tabloid press had hung on it over the last decades. The Alien Invader. The Space Fizzle. Silent Alien Cal.

"Approach for retina scan," the soldier said. Cowell wheeled his chair to the checker, leaned in close. "Okay, you're cleared. Ma'am?…Okay. Proceed." The soldier stuck his head back in the window, and the screen made one of the elaborate noises that accompanied the latest hologame.

Barbara muttered, "As if he knew the value of what he's guarding!"

"He knows," Cowell said. He didn't really want to talk to Barbara. Much as he loved her, he really would have preferred to come to this place alone. Or with Sharon, if Sharon had still been alive. But Barbara had been afraid he might have some sort of final attack alone there by the object, and of course he might have. He was pretty close to the end, and they both knew it. Getting here from Detroit was taking everything Cowell had left.

He wheeled down the paved path. On either side, autumn stubble glinted with frost. They were almost on the object before it materialized out of the fog.

Barbara began to babble. "Oh, it looks so different from pictures, even holos, so much smaller but shinier, too, you never told me it was so shiny, Dad, I guess whatever it's made of doesn't rust. But, no, of course the air isn't getting close enough to rust it, is it, there's that shield to prevent oxidation, and they never found out what *that* is composed of, either, did they, although I remember reading this speculative article that—"

Cowell shut her out as best he could. He brought his chair close enough to touch the shield. Still nothing: no tingle, no humming, no moving. Nothing at all.

That first time rushed back to him, in sharp sensory detail. The fatigue, the strain, the rustle of corn husks in the unseen wind. Hans Kleinschmidt's Styrofoam cup of coffee warm in Cowell's hand. Ann Pettie's cry *It's landing here! Run!* Cowell's own strange personal feeling of inevitability: *Of course. They wouldn't let me miss this.*

Well, they *had.* They'd let the whole world miss whatever the hell the object was supposed to be, or do, or represent. Hans was long dead. Ann was institutionalized with Alzheimer's. "*Hello, ship.*" And the rest of his life—of many people's lives—devoted to trying to figure out the Space Super Fizzle.

That long frustration, Cowell thought, had showed him one thing, anyway. There was no mystery behind the mystery, no unseen Plan, no alien messiah for humanity. There was only this blank object sitting in a field, stared at by a shrill middle-aged woman and a dying man. What you see is what you get. He, James Everett Cowell, had been a fool to ever hope for anything else.

"Dad, why are you smiling like that? Don't, please!"

"It's nothing, Barbara."

"But you looked—"

"I *said*, 'It's nothing.'"

Suddenly he was very tired. It was cold out here, under the gray sky. Snow was in the air.

"Honey, let's go back now."

They did, Barbara walking close by Cowell's chair. He didn't look back at the object, silent on the fallow ground.

Transmission: There is nothing here yet.
Current probability of occurrence: 67%.

II: 2090

THE GIRL, DRESSED IN HOME-DYED blue cotton pants and a wolf pelt bandeau, said suddenly, "Tam—what's *that*?"

Tam Wilkinson stopped walking, although his goat herd did not. The animals moved slowly forward, pulling at whatever tough grass they could find on the parched ground. Three-legged Himmie hobbled close to the herd leader; blind Jimmie turned his head in the direction of Himmie's bawl. "What's what?" the boy said.

"Over there, to the north…no, *there*."

The boy shaded his eyes against the summer sun, hot under the thin clouds. He and Juli would have to find noon shade for the goats soon. Tam's eyes weren't strong, but by squinting and peering, he caught the glint of sunlight on something dull silvery. "I don't know."

"Let's go see."

Tam looked bleakly at Juli. They had married only a few months ago, in the spring. She was so pretty, hardly any deformity at all. The doctor from St. Paul had issued her a fertility certificate at only fourteen. But she was impulsive. Tam, three years older, came from a family unbroken since the Collapse. They hadn't accomplished that by impulsive behavior.

"No, Juli. We have to find shade for the goats."

"It could *be* shade. O, or even a machine with some good metal on it!"

"This whole area was stripped long ago."

"Maybe they missed something."

Tam considered. She could be right; since their marriage, he and Juli had brought the goats pretty far beyond their usual range. Not many people had ventured into the Great Northern Waste for pasturage. The whole area had been too hard hit at the Collapse, leaving the soil too contaminated and the standing water even worse. But the summer had been unusually rainy, creating the running water that was so much safer than ponds or lakes, and anyway Tam and Juli had delighted in being alone. Maybe there *was* a forgotten machine with usable parts still sitting way out here, from before the Collapse. What a great thing to bring home from his honeymoon!

"Please," Juli said, nibbling his ear, and Tam gave in. She was so pretty. In Tam's entire family, no women were as pretty, nor as nearly whole, as Juli. His sister Nan was loose-brained, Calie had only one arm, Jen was blind, and Suze could not walk. Only Jen was fertile, even though the

Wilkinson farm was near neither lake nor city. The farm still sat in the path of the west winds coming from Grand Forks. When there had been a Grand Forks.

Tam and Juli walked slowly, herding the goats, toward the glinting metal. The sun glared pitilessly by the time they reached the object, but the thing, whatever it was, stood beside a stand of scrawny trees in a little dell. Tam drove the goats into the shade. His practiced eye saw that once there had been water here, but no longer. They would have to move on by early afternoon.

When the goats were settled, the lovers walked hand-in-hand toward the object. "O," Juli said, "it's an egg! A metal egg!" Suddenly she clutched Tam's arm. "Is it...do you think it's a polluter?"

Tam felt growing excitement. "No—I know what this is! Gran told me, before she died!"

"It's not a polluter?"

"No, it...well, actually, nobody knows exactly what it's made of. But it's safe, dear love. It's a miracle."

"A what?" Juli said.

"A miracle." He tried not to sound superior; Juli was sensitive about her lack of education. Tam was teaching her to read and write. "A gift directly from God. A long time ago—a few hundred years, I think, anyway before the Collapse—this egg fell out of the sky. No one could figure out why. Then one day a beautiful princess touched it, and she got pregnant and bore twin sons."

"Really?" Juli breathed. She ran a few steps forward, then considerately slowed for Tam's halting walk. "What happened then?"

Tam shrugged. "Nothing, I guess. The Collapse happened."

"So this egg, it just sat here since then? Come on, sweet one, I want to see it up close. It just sat here? When women try so hard, us, to get pregnant?"

The boy didn't like the skeptical tone in her voice. He was the one with the educated family. "You don't understand, Juli. This thing didn't make everybody pregnant, just that one princess. It was a special miracle from God."

"I thought you told me that before the Collapse, nobody needed no miracles to get pregnant, because there wasn't no pollutants in the water and air and ground?"

"Yes, but—"

"So then when this princess got herself pregnant, why was it such a miracle?"

"Because she was a virgin, loose-brain!" After a minute he added, "I'm sorry."

"I'm going to look at the egg," Juli said stiffly, and this time she ran ahead without waiting.

When Tam caught up, Juli was sitting cross-legged in prayer in front of the egg. It was smaller than he had expected, no bigger than a goat shed, a slightly irregular oval of dull silver. Around it the ground shimmered with heat. Minnesota hadn't always been so hot, Gran had told Tam in her papery old-lady voice, and he suddenly wondered what this place had looked like when the egg fell out of the sky.

Could it be a polluter? It didn't look like it manufactured anything, and certainly Tam couldn't see any plastic parts to it. Nothing that could flake off in bits too tiny to see and get into the air and water and wind and living bodies. Still, if they were so very small, these dangerous pieces of plastic... "endocrine mimickers," Gran had taught Tam to call them, though he had no idea what the words meant. Doctors in St. Paul knew, probably. Although what good was knowing, if you couldn't fix the problem and make all babies as whole as Juli?

She sat saying her prayer beads so fervently that Tam was annoyed with her all over again. Really, she just wasn't steady. Playful, then angry, then prayerful...she'd better be more reliable than that when the babies started to come.

But then Juli raised her eyes to him, lake-blue, and appealed to his greater knowledge, and he softened again.

"Tam...do you think it's all right to pray to it? Since it did come from God?"

"I'm sure it's all right, honey. What are you praying for?"

"Twin sons, like the princess got." Juli scrambled to her feet. "Can I touch it?"

Tam felt sudden fear. "No! No—better not. *I* will, instead." When those twin sons came, he wanted them to be of his seed, not the egg's.

Cautiously the boy put out one hand, which stopped nearly a foot away from the silvery shell. Tam pushed harder. He couldn't get any closer to the egg. "It's got an invisible wall around it!"

"Really? Then can I touch it? It's not really touching the egg!"

"No! The wall is all the princess must have touched, too."

"Maybe the wall, it wasn't there a long time ago. Maybe it grew, like crops."

Tam frowned, torn between pride and irritation at her quick thought. "Don't touch it, Juli. After all, for all we know, you might already be pregnant."

She obeyed, stepping back and studying the object. Suddenly her pretty face lit up. "Tam! Maybe it's a miracle for us, too! For the whole family!"

"The whole—"

"For Nan and Calie and Suze! And your cousins, too! O, if they come here and touch the egg—or the egg wall—maybe they can get pregnant like the princess did, straight from God!"

"I don't think—"

"If we came back before winter, in easy stages, and knowing ahead of time where the water was, they could all get pregnant! You could talk them into it, dear heart! You're the only one they listen to, even your parents. The only one who can make plans and carry out them plans. You know you are."

She looked at him with adoration. Tam felt something inside him glow and expand. And O, she really was quick, even if she couldn't read or write. His parents were old, at least forty, and they'd never been as quick as Tam. That was why Gran had taught him so much directly, all sorts of things she'd learned from her grandmother, who could remember the Collapse.

He said, with slow weightiness, "If the workers in the family stayed to raise crops, we could bring the goats and the infertile women…in easy stages, I think, before fall. Provided we map ahead of time where the safe water is."

"O, I know you can!"

Tam frowned thoughtfully, and reached out again to touch the silent, unreachable egg.

Just before the small expedition left the Wilkinson farm, Dr. Sutter showed up on his dirt bike.

Why did he have to come now? Tam didn't like Dr. Sutter, who always acted so superior. He biked around the farms and villages, supposedly "helping people"—O, he did help some people, maybe, but not Tam's family, who *were* their village. Not really helped. O, he'd brought drugs for Gran's aching bones, and for Suze's fever, from the hospital in St. Paul. But he hadn't been able to stop Tam's sisters—or anybody else—from being born the way they were, and not all his "medical training" could make Suze or Nan or Calie fertile. And Dr. Sutter lorded it over Tam, who otherwise was the smartest person in the family.

"I'm afraid," Suze said. She rode the family mule; the others walked. Suze and Calie; Nan, led by Tam's cousin Jack; Uncle Seddie and Uncle Ned, both armed; Tam and Juli. Juli stood talking, sparkly eyed, to Sutter. To Tam's disappointment, no baby had been started on the honeymoon.

He said, "Nothing to be afraid of, Suze. Juli! Time to go!"

She danced over to him. "Dave's coming, too! He says he got a few weeks' vacation and would like to see the egg. He knows about it, Tam!"

Of course he did. Tam set his lips together and didn't answer.

"He says it's from people on another world, not from God, and—"

"My gran said it was from God," Tam said sharply. At his tone, Juli stopped walking.

"Tam—"

"I'll speak to Sutter myself. Telling you these city lies. Now go walk by Suze. She's afraid."

Juli, eyes no longer sparkling, obeyed. Tam told himself he was going to go over and have this out with Sutter, just as soon as he got everything going properly. Of *course* the egg was from God! Gran had said so, and anyway, if it wasn't, what was the point of this whole expedition, taking workers away from the farm, even if it was the mid-summer quiet between planting and harvest.

But somehow, with one task and another, Tam didn't find time to confront Sutter until night, when they were camped by the first lake. Calie and Suze slept, and the others sat around a comfortable fire, full of corn mush and fresh rabbit. Somewhere in the darkness, a wolf howled.

"Lots more of those than when I was young," said Uncle Seddie, who was almost seventy. "Funny thing, too—when you trap 'em, they're hardly ever deformed. Not like rabbits or frogs. Frogs, they're the worst."

Sutter said, "Wolves didn't move back down to Minnesota until after the Collapse. Up in Canada, they weren't as exposed to endocrine-mimicking pollutants. And frogs have always been the worst; water animals are especially sensitive to environmental factors."

Some of the words were the same ones Gran had used, but that didn't make Tam like them any better. He didn't know what they meant, and he wasn't about to ask Sutter.

Juli did, though. "Those endo...endo...what are they, doctor?"

He smiled at her, his straight white teeth gleaming in the firelight. "Environmental pollutants that bind to receptor sites all over the body, disrupting its normal function. They especially affect fetuses. Just before the Collapse, they reached some sort of unanticipated critical mass, and suddenly there were worldwide fertility problems, neurological impairments, cerebral.... Sorry, Juli, you got me started on my medical diatribe. I mean, pretty lady, that too few babies were born, and too many of those who were born couldn't think or move right, and we had the Collapse."

Beside him, Nan, born loose-brained, crooned softly to herself.

Juli said innocently, "But I thought the Collapse, it came from wars and money and bombs and things like that."

"Yes," Sutter said, "but those things happened *because* of the population and neurological problems."

"O, I'm just glad I didn't live then!" Ned said, shuddering. "It must have been terrible, especially in the cities."

Juli said, "But, doctor, aren't you from a city?"

Sutter looked into the flames. The wolf howled again. "Some cities fared much better than others. We *lost* most of the East Coast, you know, to various terrorist wars, and—"

"Everybody knows that," Tam said witheringly.

Sutter was undeterred, "—and California to rioting and looting. But St. Paul came through, eventually. And a basic core of knowledge and skills persisted, even if only in the urban areas. Science, medicine, engineering. We don't have the skilled population, or even a neurologically functional population, but we haven't really gone pre-industrial. There are even pockets of research, especially in biology. We'll beat this, someday."

"I know we will!" Juli said, her eyes shining. She was always so optimistic. Like a child, not a grown woman.

Tam said, "And meanwhile, the civilized types like you graciously go around to the poor country villages that feed you and bless them with your important skills."

Sutter looked at him across the fire. "That's right, Tam."

Uncle Seddie said, "Enough arguing. Go to bed, everybody."

Seddie was the ranking elder; there was no choice but to obey. Tam pulled Juli up with him, and in their bedroll he copulated with her so hard that she had to tell him to be more gentle, he was hurting her.

They reached the egg, by the direct route Tam had mapped out, in less than a week. Another family already camped beside it.

The two approached each other warily, guns and precious ammunition prominently displayed. But the other family, the Janeways, turned out to be a lot like the Wilkinsons, a goat-and-farm clan whose herdsmen had discovered the egg and brought others back to see the God-given miracle.

Tam, standing behind Seddie and Ned, said, "There's some that don't think it is from God."

The ranking Janeway, a tough old woman lean as Gran had been, said sharply, "Where else could it come from, way out here? No city tech left this here."

"That's what we say," Seddie answered. He lowered his rifle. "You people willing to trade provisions? We got maple syrup, corn mush, some good pepper."

"Pepper?" The old woman's eyes brightened. "You got pepper?"

"We trade with a family that trades in St. Paul," Ned said proudly. "Twice a year, spring and fall."

"We got sugar and an extra radio."

Tam's chin jerked up. A radio! But that was worth more than any amount of provisions. Nobody would casually trade a radio.

"Our family runs to boys, nearly all boys," the old woman said, by way of explanation. She looked past Tam, at Juli and Calie and Suze and Nan, hanging back with the mule and backpacks. "They're having trouble finding fertile wives. If any of your girls…and if the young people liked each other…"

"Juli, the blond, she's married to Tam here," Seddie said. "And the other girls, they aren't fertile…*yet.*"

"'Yet'? What do you mean, 'yet'?"

Seddie pointed with his rifle at the egg. "Don't you know what that is?"

"A gift from God," the woman said.

"Yes. But don't you know about the princess and her twins? Tell her, Tam."

Tam told the story, feeling himself thrill to it as he did so. The woman listened intently, then squinted again at the girls. Seddie said quickly, "Nan is loose-brained, I have to tell you. And Suze is riding because her foot is crippled, although she's got the sweetest, meekest nature you could ever find. But Calie there, even though she's got a withered arm, is quick and smart and can do almost anything. And after she touches the egg…. but, ma'am, Wilkinsons don't force marriages on our women. Never. Calie'd have to like one of your sons, and want to go with you."

"O, we can see what happens," the woman said, and winked, and for a second Tam saw what she must have been once, long ago, on a sweet summer night like this one when she was young.

He said suddenly, "The girls have to touch the egg at dawn."

Seddie and Ned turned to him. "Dawn? Why dawn?"

Tam didn't know why he'd said that, but now he had to see it through. "I don't know. God just made that idea come to me."

Seddie said to Mrs. Janeway, "Tam's our smartest person. Always has been."

"All right, then. Dawn."

In the chill morning light, the girls lined up, shivering. Mrs. Janeway, Dr. Sutter, and the men from both families made an awkward semicircle around them, shuffling their feet a little, not looking at each other. The five Janeway boys, a tangle of uncles and cousins, all looked a bit stooped, but they could all walk, and none were loose-brained. Tam had spent the previous evening at the communal campfire, saying little, watching and listening to see which Janeways might be good to his sisters. He'd already decided that Cal had a temper, and if he asked Uncle Seddie for Calie or Suze, Tam would advise against it.

Dr. Sutter had said nothing at the campfire, listening to the others become more and more excited about the egg-touching, about the fertility from God. Even when Mrs. Janeway had asked him questions, his replies had been short and evasive. She'd kept watching him, clearly suspicious. Tam had liked her more and more as the long evening progressed.

Followed by a longer night. Tam and Juli had argued.

"I want to touch it, too, Tam."

"No. You have your certificate from that doctor two years ago. She tested you, and you're already fertile."

"Then why haven't I started no baby? Maybe the fertility went away."

"It doesn't do that."

"How do you know? I asked Dr. Sutter and he said—"

"You told Dr. Sutter about your body?" Rage swamped Tam.

Juli's voice grew smaller. "O, he *is* a doctor! Tam, he says it's hard to be sure about fertility testing for women, the test is…is some word I don't remember. But he says about one certificate in four is wrong. He says we should do away with the certificates. He says—"

"I don't care what he says!" Tam had all but shouted. "I don't want you talking to him again! If I see you are, Juli, I'll take it up with Uncle Seddie. And you are not touching the egg!"

Juli had raised herself on one elbow to stare at him in the starlight, then had turned her back and pretended to sleep until dawn.

Now she led Nan, the oldest sister, toward the egg. Nan crooned, drooling a little, and smiled at Juli. Juli was always tender with Nan. She smiled back, wiped Nan's chin, and guided her hand toward the silvery oval. Tam watched carefully to see that Juli didn't touch the egg herself. She didn't, and neither did Nan, technically, since her hand stopped at whatever unseen wall protected the object. But everyone let out a sharp breath, and Nan laughed suddenly, one of her clear high giggles, and Tam felt suddenly happier.

Seddie said, "Now Suze."

Juli led Nan away. Suze, carried by Uncle Ned, reached out and touched the egg. She, too, laughed aloud, her sweet face alight, and Tam saw Vic Janeway lean forward a little, watching her. Suze couldn't plow or plant, but she was the best cook in the family if everything were put in arm's reach. And she could sew and weave and read and carve.

Next Calie, pretty if Juli hadn't been there for comparison, and the other four Janeway men watched. Calie's one hand, dirt under the small fingernails, stayed on the egg a long time, trembling.

No one spoke.

"O, then," Mrs. Janeway said, "we should pray."

They did, each family waiting courteously while the other said their special prayers, all joining in the "Our Father." Tam caught Sutter looking at him somberly, and he glared back. Nothing Sutter's "medicine" had ever done had helped Tam's sisters, and anyway, it was none of Sutter's business what the Wilkinsons and Janeways did. Let him go back to St. Paul with his heathen beliefs.

"I want to touch the egg," Juli said. "I won't get no other chance. We leave in the morning."

Tam had had no idea that she could be so stubborn. She'd argued and pleaded for the three days they'd camped with the Janeways, letting the families get to know each other. Now they were leaving in the morning, with Vic and Lenny Janeway traveling with them to stay until the end of harvest, so Suze and Calie could decide about marriage. And Juli was still arguing!

"I said no," Tam said tightly. He was afraid to say more—afraid not of her, but of himself. Some men beat their wives; not Wilkinson men. But watching Juli all evening, Tam had suddenly understood those other men. She had deliberately sat talking only to Dr. Sutter, smiling at him in the flickering firelight. Even Uncle Ned had noticed, Tam thought, and that made Tam writhe with shame. He had dragged Juli off to bed early, and here she was arguing still, while singing started around the fire twenty feet away.

"Tam...please! I want to start a baby, and nothing we do started one.... Don't get upset, but...but Dr. Sutter says sometimes the man is infertile, even though it don't happen as often as women's wombs it can still happen, and maybe—"

It was too much. First his wife shames him by spending the evening sitting close to another man, talking and laughing, and then she suggests that *him*, not her, might be the reason there was no baby yet. Him! When God had clearly closed the wombs of women after the Collapse, just like he did to those sinning women in the Bible! Anger and shame thrilled through Tam, and before he knew he was going to do it, he hit her.

It was only a slap. Juli put her hand to her cheek, and Tam suddenly would have given everything he possessed to take the slap back. Juli jumped up and ran off in the darkness, away from the fire. Tam let her go. She had a right to be upset now, he'd given her that. He lay stiffly in the darkness, intending every second to go get her—there were wolves out there, after all, although they seldom attacked people. Still, he would go get her. But he didn't, and, without knowing it, he fell asleep.

When he woke, it was near dawn. Juli woke him, creeping back into their bedroll.

"Juli! You…it's nearly dawn. Where were you all this time?"

She didn't answer. In the icy pale light, her face was flushed.

He said slowly, "You touched it."

She wriggled the rest of the way into the bedroll and turned her back to him. Over her shoulder she said, "No, Tam. I didn't touch it."

"You're lying to me."

"No. I didn't touch it," she repeated, and Tam believed her. So he had won. Generosity filled him.

"Juli—I'm sorry I hit you. So sorry."

Abruptly she twisted in the bedroll to face him. "I know. Tam, listen to me…God wants me to start a baby. He does!"

"Yes, of course," Tam said, bewildered by her sudden ferocity.

"He wants me to start a baby!"

"Are you…are you saying that you have?"

She was silent a long time. Then she said, "Yes. I think so."

Joy filled him. He took her in his arms, and she let him. It would all be right, now. He and Juli would have a child, many children. So would Suze and Calie, and—who could say?—maybe even Nan. The egg's fame would grow, and there would be many babies again.

On the journey home, Juli stuck close to Tam, never looking even once in Dr. Sutter's direction. He avoided her, too. Tam gloated; so much for science and tech from the cities! When they reached the farm, Dr. Sutter retrieved his dirt bike and rode away. The next time a doctor came to call, it was someone different.

Juli bore a girl, strong and whole except for two missing fingers. During her marriage to Tam, she bore four more children, finally dying while trying to deliver a sixth one. Suze and Calie married the Janeway boys, but neither conceived. After three years of trying, Lenny Janeway sent Calie back to the Wilkinsons; Calie never smiled or laughed much again.

For decades afterward, the egg was proclaimed a savior, a gift from God, a miracle to repopulate Minnesota. Families came and feasted and prayed, and the girls touched the egg, more each year. Most of the girls never started a baby, but a few did, and at times the base of the egg was almost invisible under the gifts of flowers, fruit, woven cloth, even a computer from St. Paul and a glass perfume bottle from much farther away, so delicate that the wind smashed it one night. Or bears did, or maybe even angels. Some people said that angels visited the egg regularly. They said that the angels even touched it, through the invisible wall.

Tam's oldest daughter didn't believe that. She didn't believe much, Tam thought, for she was the great disappointment of his life. Strong, beautiful, smart, she got herself accepted to a merit school in St. Paul, and she went, despite her missing fingers. She made herself into a scientist and turned her back on the Bible. Tam, who had turned more stubborn as he grew old, refused to see her again. She said that the egg wasn't a miracle and had never made anyone pregnant. She said there were no saviors for humanity but itself.

Tam, who had become not only more stubborn but also more angry after Juli died, turned his face away and refused to listen.

Transmission: There is nothing here yet.
Current probability of occurrence: 28%.

III: 2175

Abby4 said, "The meeting is in *northern Minnesota*? Why?"

Mal held onto his temper. He'd been warned about Abby4. *One of the Biomensas*, Mal's network of friends and colleagues had said, *In the top 2 percent of genemods. She likes to throw around her superiority. Don't let her twist you. The contract is too important.*

His friends had also said not to be intimidated by either Abby4's office or her beauty. The office occupied the top floor of the tallest building in Raleigh, with a sweeping view of the newly cleaned-up city. A garden in the sky, its walls and ceiling were completely hidden by the latest genemod plants from AbbyWorks, flowers so exotic and brilliant that, just looking at them, a visitor could easily forget what he was going to say. Probably that was the idea.

Abby4's beauty was even more distracting than her office. She sat across from him in a soft white chair that only emphasized her sleek, hard glossiness. The face of an Aztec princess, framed by copper hair pulled into a thick roll on either side. The sash of her black business suit stopped just above the swell of white breasts that Mal determinedly ignored. Her legs were longer than his dreams.

Mal said pleasantly, "The meeting is in northern Minnesota because the Chinese contact is already doing business in St. Paul, at the university. And he wants to see a curiosity near the old Canadian border, an object that government records show as an alien artifact."

Abby4 blinked, probably before she knew that she was going to do it, which gave Mal enormous satisfaction. Not even the Biomensas, with their genetically engineered intelligence and memory, knew everything.

"Ah, yes, of course," Abby4 said, and Mal was careful not to recognize the bluff. "O, then, northern Minnesota. Send my office system the details, please. Thank you, Mr. Goldstone."

Mal rose to go. Abby4 did not rise. In the outer office, he passed a woman several years older than Abby4 but looking so much like her that it must be one of the earlier clones. The woman stooped slightly. Undoubtedly each successive clone had better genemods as the technology came onto the market. AbbyWorks was, after all, one of the five or six leading biosolutions companies in Raleigh, and that meant in the world.

Mal left the Eden-like AbbyWorks building to walk into the shrouding heat of a North Carolina summer. In the parking lot, his car wouldn't start. Cursing, he opened the hood. Someone had broken the hood lock and stolen the engine.

Purveyors of biosolutions to the world, Mal thought bitterly, cleaners-up of the ecological, neurological, and population disasters of the Collapse, and we still can't create a decent hood lock! O, that actually figured. For the last hundred and fifty years—no, closer to two hundred now—the best minds of each American generation had been concentrating on biology. Engineering, physics, and everything else got few practitioners, and even less funding.

O, it had paid off. Not only for people like Abby4, the beautiful Biomensa bitch, but even for comparative drones like Mal. He had biological defenses against lingering environmental pollutants (they would linger for another thousand years), he was fertile, he even had modest genemods so that he didn't look like a troll or think like a troglodyte. What he *didn't* have was a working car.

He took out his phone and called a cab.

August in Minnesota was not cold, but Kim Mao Xun, the Chinese client, was well wrapped in layers of silk and thin wool. He looked very old, which meant that he was probably even older. Obviously no genemods for appearance, Mal thought, whatever else Mr. Kim might have. O, they did things differently in China! When you survived the Collapse on nothing but sheer numbers, you started your long climb back with essentials, nothing else.

"I am so excited to see the Alien Craft," he said in excellent English. "It is famous in China, you know."

Abby4 smiled. "Here, I'm afraid, it's mostly a curiosity. Very few people even know it exists, although the government has authenticated from written records that it landed in October 2007, an event widely recorded by the best scientific instruments of the age."

"So much better than what we have now," Mr. Kim murmured, and Abby4 frowned.

"O, yes, I suppose…but then, they didn't have a world to clean up, did they?"

"And we do. Mr. Goldstone tells me you can help us do this in Shanghai."

"Yes, we can," Abby4 said, and the meeting began to replicate in earnest.

Mal listened intently, taking notes, but said nothing. Meeting brokers didn't get involved in details. Matching, arranging, follow-through, impartial evaluation, and, if necessary, arbitration. Then disappear until the next time. But Mal was interested; this was his biggest client so far.

And the biggest problem: Shanghai. The city and the harbor, which must add up to hundreds of different pollutants, each needing a different genetically designed organism to attack it. Plus, Shanghai had been viral-bombed during the war with Japan. Those viruses would be much mutated by now, especially if they had jumped hosts, which they probably had. Mal could see that even Abby4 was excited by the scope of the job, although she was trying to conceal it.

"What is Shanghai's current population, Mr. Kim?"

"Zero." Mr. Kim smiled wryly. "Officially, anyway. The city is quarantined. Of course, there are the usual stoopers and renegades, but we will do our best to relocate them before you begin, and those who will not go may be ignored by your operators."

Something chilling in that. Although did the US do any better? Mal had heard stories—everyone had heard stories—of families who'd stayed in the most contaminated areas for generations, becoming increasingly deformed and increasingly frightening. There were even people still living in places like New York City, which had taken the triple blow of pollutants, bioweapons, and radiation. Theoretically, the population of New York City was zero. In reality, nobody would go in to count, nor even send in the doggerels, biosolutioned canines with magnitude-one immunity and selectively enhanced intelligence. A doggerel was too expensive to risk in New York. Whoever—or whatever—couldn't be counted by robots (and American robots were so inadequate compared to the Asian product), stayed uncounted.

"I understand," Abby4 said to Mr. Kim. "And the time-frame?"

"We would like to have Shanghai totally clean ten years from now."

Abby4's face didn't change. "That is very soon."

"Yes. Can you do it?"

"I need to consult with my scientists," she said, and Mal felt his chest fill with lightness. She hadn't said no, and when Abby4 didn't say no, the answer was likely to be yes. The ten-year deadline—only ten years!—would make the fee enormous, and Mal's company's small percentage of it would rise accordingly. A promotion, a bonus, a new car....

"Then until I hear back from you, we can go no farther," Mr. Kim said. "Shall we take my car to the Alien Craft?"

"Certainly," Abby4 said. "Mr. Goldstone? Can you accompany us? I'm told you know exactly where this curious object is." *As a busy and important Biomensa executive like me would not*, was the unstated message, but Mal didn't mind. He was too happy.

The Alien Craft, as Mr. Kim persisted in calling it, was not easy to find. Northern Minnesota had all been cleaned up, of course; as valuable farm and dairy land, it had had priority, and anyway, the damage hadn't been too bad. But, once cleaned, the agrisolution companies wanted the place for farming, free of outside interference. The government, the weak partner in all that biotech corporations did, reluctantly agreed. The Alien Craft lay under an inconspicuous foamcast dome at the end of an obscure road, with no identifying signs of any kind.

Mal saw immediately why Mr. Kim had suggested going in his car, which had come with him from China. The Chinese were forced to buy all their biosolutions from others. In compensation, they had created the finest engineering and hard-goods manufactories in the world. Mr. Kim's car was silent, fast, and computer-driven, technology unknown in the United States. Mal could see that even Abby4 was unwillingly impressed.

He leaned back against the contoured seats, which molded themselves to his body, and watched farmland flash past at an incredible rate. There were government officials and university professors who said that the United States should fear Chinese technology, even if it wasn't based on biology. Maybe they were right.

In contrast, the computer-based security at the Alien Craft looked primitive. Mal had arranged for entry, and they passed through the locks into the dome, which was only ten feet wider on all sides than the Alien Craft itself. Mal had never seen it before, and despite himself, he was impressed.

The Craft was dull silver, as big as a small bedroom, a slightly irregular oval. In the artificial light of the dome, it shimmered. When Mal put out a hand to touch it, his hand stopped almost a foot away.

"A force field of some unknown kind, unknown even before the Collapse," Abby4 said, with such authority you'd think she'd done field tests herself. "The shield extends completely around the Craft, even below ground, where it is also impenetrable. The Craft was very carefully monitored in the decades between its landing and the Collapse, and never once did any detectable signal of any kind go out from it. No outgoing signals, no aliens disembarking, no outside markings to decode…no communication of any kind. One wonders why the aliens bothered to send it at all."

Mr. Kim quoted, "'The wordless teaching, the profit in not doing—not many people understand it.'"

"Ah," Abby4 said, too smart to either agree or disagree with a philosophy—Taoist? Buddhist?—she patently didn't share.

Mal walked completely around the Craft, wondering himself why anybody would bother with such a tremendous undertaking without any follow-up. Of course, maybe it hadn't been tremendous to the *aliens*. Maybe they sent interstellar silvery metal ovals to other planets all the time without follow-up. But *why*?

When Mal reached his starting point in the circular dome, Mr. Kim was removing an instrument from his leather bag.

Mal had never seen an instrument like it, but then, he'd hardly seen any scientific instruments at all. This one looked like a flat television, with a glass screen on one side, metal on the other five. Only the "glass" clearly *wasn't*, since it seemed to shift as Mr. Kim lifted it, as if it were a field of its own. As Mal watched, Mr. Kim applied the field side of the device onto the side of the Craft, where it stayed even as he stepped back.

Mal said uncertainly, "I don't think you should—"

Abby4 said, "O, it doesn't matter, Mr. Goldstone. Nothing anyone has ever done has penetrated the Craft's force field, even before the Collapse."

Mr. Kim just smiled.

Mal said, "You don't understand. The clearance I arranged with the State Department…it doesn't include taking any readings or…or whatever that device is doing. Mr. Kim?"

"Just taking some readings," Mr. Kim said blandly.

Mal's unease grew. "Please stop. As I say, I didn't obtain clearances for this!"

Abby4 scowled at him fiercely. Mr. Kim said, "Of course, Mr. Goldstone," and detached his device. "I am sorry to alarm you. Just some readings. Shall we go now? A most interesting object, but rather monotonous."

On the way back to St. Paul, Mr. Kim and Abby4 discussed the historic cleanups of Boston, Paris, and Lisbon, as if nothing had happened.

What had?

AbbyWorks got the Shanghai contract. Mal got his promotion, his bonus, and his new car. Someone else handled the follow-up for the contract while Mal went on to new projects, but every so often, he checked to see how the clean-up of Shanghai was proceeding. Two years into the agreement, the job was actually ahead of projected schedule, despite badly deteriorating relations between the two countries. China invaded and annexed Tibet, but China had *always* invaded and annexed Tibet, and only the human-solidarity people objected. Next, however, China annexed the Kamchatka Peninsula, where American biosolutions companies were working on the clean-up of Vladivostock. The genemod engineers brought back frightening stories of advanced Chinese engineering: room-temperature superconductors. Maglev trains. Nanotechnology. There were even rumors of quantum computers, capable of handling trillions of operations simultaneously, although Mal discounted those rumors completely. A practical quantum computer was still far over the horizon.

AbbyWorks was ordered out of Shanghai by the United States government. The company did not leave. Abby1 was jailed, but this made no difference. The Shanghai profits were paid to offshore banks. AbbyWorks claimed to have lost control of its Shanghai employees, who were making huge personal fortunes, enough to enable them to live outside the United States for the rest of very luxurious lives. Then, abruptly, the Chinese government itself terminated the contract. They literally threw AbbyWorks out of China in the middle of the night. They kept for themselves enormous resources in patented scientific equipment, as well as monies due for the last three months' work, an amount equal to some state budgets.

At three o'clock in the morning, Mal received a visit from the Office of National Security.

"Mallings Goldstone?"

"Yes?"

"We need to ask you some questions."

Recorders, intimidation. The ONS had information that in 2175 Mr. Goldstone had conducted two people to the Minnesota site of the space object: Abby4 Abbington, president of AbbyWorks Biosolutions, and Mr. Kim Mao Xun of the Chinese government.

"Yes, I did," Mal said, sitting stiffly in his nightclothes. "It's on record. I had proper clearances."

"Yes. But during that visit, did Mr. Kim take out and attach to the space object an unknown device, and then return it to his briefcase?"

"Yes." Mal's stomach twisted.

"Why wasn't this incident reported to the State Department?"

"I didn't think it was important." Not entirely true. Abby4 must have reported it…but why *now*? Because of the lost monies and confiscated equipment, of course. Adding to the list of Chinese treacheries; a longer list was more likely to compel government reaction.

"Do you have any idea what the device was, or what it might have done to the space object?"

"No."

"Then you didn't rule out that its effects might have been dangerous to your country?"

"'Dangerous'? How?"

"We don't know, Mr. Mallings—that's the point. We do know that in nonbiological areas the Chinese technology is far ahead of our own. We have no way of knowing if that device you failed to report turned the space object into a weapon of some kind."

"A weapon? Don't you think that's very unlikely?"

"No, Mr. Mallings. I don't. Please get dressed and come with us."

For the first time, Mal noticed the two men's builds. Genemod for strength and agility, no doubt, as well as maximum possible longevity. He remembered Mr. Kim, scrawny and wrinkled. Their bodies far outclassed Mr. Kim's, far outclassed Mal's as well. But Mr. Kim's body was somewhere on the other side of the world, along with his superior "devices," and Mal's body was marked "scapegoat" as clearly as if it were spelled out in DNA-controlled birth-marks on his forehead.

He went into his bedroom to get dressed.

Mal had been interrogated with truth drugs—painless, harmless, utterly reliable—recorded, and released by the time the news hit the flimsies. He had already handed in his resignation to his company. The moving truck stood outside his apartment, being loaded for the move to someplace he wasn't known. Mal, flimsy in hand, watched the two huge stevies carry out his furniture.

But he couldn't postpone reading the flimsy forever. And, of course, this was just the first. There would be more. The tempaper rustled in his hand. It would last forty-eight hours before dissolving into molecules completely harmless to the environment.

CHINESE ARMED "SPACE OBJECT" TO DESTROY US!!!

"MIGHT BE RADIATION, OR POLLUTANTS, OR A SUPER-BOMB," SAY SCIENTISTS

TROJAN HORSE UNDER GUISE OF BIOSOLUTIONS CONTRACT

TWO YEARS AND NOTHING HAS BEEN DONE!!!!

Flimsies weren't subtle. But so far as Mal could see, his name hadn't yet been released to them.

Mal said, "Please be careful with that desk, it's very old. It belonged to my great-grandfather."

"O, yes, friend," one of the stevies said. "Most careful." They hurled it into the truck.

A neighbor of Mal's walked toward Mal, recognized him, and stopped dead. She hissed at him, a long ugly sound, and walked on.

So some other flimsy had already tracked him down and published his name.

"Leave the rest," Mal said suddenly, "everything else inside the house. Let's go."

"O, just a few crates," said one stevie.

"No, leave it." Mal climbed into the truck's passenger cubicle. He hoped that he wasn't a coward, but like all meeting brokers he was an historian, and he remembered the historical accounts of the "Anti-Polluters' Riots" of the Collapse. What those mobs had done to anyone suspected of contributing to the destruction of the environment…Mal pulled the curtains closed in the cubicle. "Let's go!"

"O, yes!" the stevies said cheerfully, and drove off.

Mal moved five states away, pursued all the way by flimsies. He couldn't change his retinal scan or DNA ID, of course, but he used a legal corporate alias with the new landlord, the grocery broker, the bank. He read the news every day, and listened to it on public radio, and it progressed as any meeting broker could foresee it would.

First, set the agenda: Demonize the Chinese, spread public fear. Second, canvass negotiating possibilities: Will they admit it? What can we contribute? Third, eliminate the possibilities you don't like and hone in on the one you do: If the United States has been attacked, it has the right to counterattack. Fourth, build in safeguards against failure: We can't yet attack China, they'll destroy us. We *can* attack the danger they've placed within our borders, and then declare victory for that. Fifth, close the deal.

The evacuation started two weeks later, and covered most of northern Minnesota and great swathes of southern Ontario. It included people and farm animals, but not wildlife, which would, of course, be replaced from cloned embryos. As the agrisolution inhabitants, many protesting furiously, were trucked out, the timed-release drops of engineered organisms were trucked in. Set loose after the bomb, they would spread over the entire affected area and disassemble all radioactive molecules. They were the same biosolutions that had cleaned up Boston, the very best AbbyWorks could create. In five years, Minnesota would be as sweet and clean as Kansas.

Or Shanghai.

The entire nation, Mal included, watched the bomb drop on vid. People held patriotic parties; wine and beer flowed. We were showing the Chinese that they couldn't endanger us in our own country! Handsome genemod news speakers, who looked like Viking princesses or Zulu warriors or Greek gods, speculated on what the space object might reveal when it was blasted open. If anything survived, of course, which was not likely…and here scientists, considerably less gorgeous than the news speakers, explained fusion and the core of the sun. The bomb might be antiquated technology, they said, but it was still workable, and would save us from Chinese perfidy.

Not to mention, Mal thought, saving face for the United States and lost revenues for AbbyWorks. It might not earn them as much to clean up Minnesota as to clean up Shanghai, but it was still a lot of money.

The bomb fell, hit the space object, and sent up a mushroom cloud. When it cleared, the object lay there exactly as before.

Airborne robots went in, spraying purifying organisms as they went, recording every measurement possible. Scientists compared the new data about the space object to the data they already had. Not one byte differed. When robotic arms reached out to touch the object, the arms still stopped ten inches away at an unseen, unmoved force field of some type not even the Chinese understood.

Mal closed his eyes. How long would Chinese retaliation take? What would they do, and when?

They did nothing. Slowly, public opinion swung to their side, helped by the flimsies. Journalists and viddies, ever eager for the next story, discovered that AbbyWorks had falsified reports on the clean-up of Shanghai. It had not been progressing as the corporation said, or as the contract promised. Eventually, AbbyWorks—already too rich, too powerful, for many people's tastes—became the villain. They had tried to frame the Chinese, who were merely trying to do normal clean-up of their part of the planet. Clean-up was our job, our legacy, our sacred stewardship of the living Earth! And anyway, Chinese technological consumer goods, increasingly available in the United States, were so much better than ours—shouldn't we be trying to learn from them?

So business partnerships were formed. The fragile Chinese-American alliance was strengthened. AbbyWorks was forced to move offshore. Mal, in some way he didn't quite understand, became a cult hero. Mr. Kim would have, too, but shortly after the bomb was dropped on the space object, he died of a heart attack, not having the proper genemods to clear out plaque from his ancient cardiac arteries.

When Minnesota was clean again, the space object went back under a new foamcast dome, and in two more generations, only historians remembered what it may or may not have saved.

Transmission: There is nothing here yet.
Current probability of occurrence: 78%.

IV:2264

FEW PEOPLE UNDERSTOOD WHY KimWorks was built in such a remote place. Dr. Leila Jian-fen Kim was one of the few who did.

She liked family history. Didn't Lao Tzu himself say, "To know what endures is to be openhearted, magnanimous, regal, blessed"? Family endures, family history endures. It was the same reason she liked the meditation garden at Kim-Works, which was where she headed now with her great secret, to compose her mind.

They had done it. Created the programmable replicator. One of the two great prizes hovering on the engineering horizon, and KimWorks had captured it.

Walking away from the sealed lab, Leila tried to empty her mind, to put the achievement to one side and let the mystery flow in. The replicator must be kept in perspective, in its rightful place. Calming herself in the meditation garden would help her remember that.

The garden was her favorite part of KimWorks. It lay at the northern end of the vast walled complex, separated from the first security fence by a simple curve of white stone. From the stone benches, you couldn't see security fences, or even most of the facility buildings. So cleverly designed was the meditation garden that no matter where you sat, you contemplated only serene things. A single blooming bush, surrounded by raked gravel. A rock, placed to catch the sun. The stream, flowing softly, living water, always seeking its natural level. Or the egg, mystery of mysteries.

It was the egg, unexplained symbol of unexplained realms beyond Earth, that brought Leila the deepest peace.

She had sat for hours when the replicator project was in its planning stage, contemplating the egg's dull silvery oval, letting her mind empty of all else. From that, she was convinced, had come most of the project's form. Form was only a temporary manifestation of the ten thousand things, and in the egg's unknowability lay the secret of its power.

Her great-grandfather, Kim Mao Xun, had known that power. He had seen the egg on an early trip to the United States, before the Alliance, even. His son had made the same visit, and his granddaughter, Leila's mother, had chosen the spot for this KimWorks facility and had the meditation garden built at its heart. Leila's father, Paul Wilkinson, had gently teased his wife about putting a garden in a scientific research center, but Father was an American. They did not always understand. With the wiser in the world lies the responsibility for teaching the less wise.

But it had been Father who had inspired Leila to become a scientist, not a businessman like her brother or a political leader like her sister. Father, were he still alive, would be proud of her now. Pride was a temptation, even pride in one's children, but it nonetheless warmed Leila's heart.

She sat, a slim, middle-aged, Chinese-born woman with smooth black hair, dressed in a blue lab coverall, and thought about the nature of pride.

The programmable replicator, unlike its predecessors, would not be limited to nanocreating a single specific molecule. It was good to be able to create any molecule you needed or wanted, of course. The extant replicators, shaped by Chinese technology, had changed the face of the Earth. Theoretically, everyone now alive could be fed, housed, clad by nanotech. But in addition to the inevitable political and economic problems of access, the existing nanotech processes were expensive. One must create the assemblers, including their tiny self-contained programs; use the assemblers to create molecules; use other techniques, chemical or mechanical, to join the molecules into products.

Now all that would change. The new KimWorks programmable replicator didn't carry assembly instructions hardwired into it. Rather, it carried programmable computers that could build anything desired, including more of themselves, from the common materials of the earth. Every research lab in the world had been straining toward this goal. And Leila's team had accomplished it.

She sat on the bench closest to the egg. The sky arched above her, for the electromagnetic dome protecting Kim-Works was invisible. Clear space had been left all around the object, except for a small flat stone visible from Leila's bench. On the stone was engraved a verse from the *Tao Te Ching*, in both Chinese and English:

THE WORDLESS TEACHING

THE PROFIT IN NOT DOING—

NOT MANY PEOPLE UNDERSTAND IT.

Certainly, in all humility, Leila didn't. Why send this egg from somewhere in deep space and have it do nothing for two and a half centuries? But that was the mystery, the power of the egg. That was why contemplating it filled her with peace.

The others were still in nanoteam one's lab building. Not many others; robots did all the routine work, of course, and only David and Chunquing and Rulan remained at the computers and stafils. It had taken Leila ten minutes to pass through the lab safeties, but she had suddenly wearied of the celebrations, the Chilean wine and holo congratulations from the CEO in Shanghai, who was her great-uncle. She had wanted to sit quietly in the cool sweet air of the garden, watching the long Minnesota twilight turn purple behind the egg. Shadow and curve, it was almost a poem....

The lab blew up.

The blast threw Leila off her bench and onto the ground. She screamed and threw up one arm to shield her eyes. But it wasn't necessary; she was shielded from direct line with the lab by the egg. And a part of her mind knew that there was no radiation anyway, only heat, and no flying debris, because the lab had imploded, as it was constructed to do. Something had breached the outer layers of sensors, and, in response, the ignition layer had produced a gas of metal oxides hot enough to vaporize everything inside the lab. No uncontrolled replicator must ever escape.

To vaporize everything. The lab. The project. David, Chunquing, Rulan.

Already, the site would be cooling. Leila staggered to her feet, and immediately was again knocked off them by an aftershock. It had been an earthquake, then, least likely of anticipated penetrations, but nonetheless guarded against. O, David, Chunquing, Rulan…

"Dr. Kim! Are you all right?!" Keesha Ali, running toward her from Security. As her ears cleared, Leila heard the sirens and alarms.

"Yes, I…Keesha!"

"I know," the woman said grimly. "Who was inside?"

"David. Chunquing. Rulan. And the replicator project… an earthquake! Of all the bad luck of heaven…"

"It wasn't bad luck," Keesha said. "We were attacked."

"Attacked—"

"That was no natural quake. Security picked up the charge just seconds before it went off. In a tunnel underneath the lab, very deep, very huge. It not only breached the lab, it destroyed the dome equipment. We're bringing the back-up online now. Meeting in Amenities in five minutes, Dr. Kim."

Leila stared at Keesha. The woman was American, of course, born here, with no Chinese ancestry. But surely even such people first mourned their dead...Yes. They did, under normal circumstances. So something extraordinary was happening here.

Leila was genemod for intelligence. She said slowly, "Data escaped."

"In the fraction of a second between breach and ignition," Keesha said grimly, "while the dome was down, including, of course, the Faraday cage. They took the entire replicator project, Dr. Kim."

Leila understood what that meant, and her mind staggered under the burden. It meant that someone else had captured the other shimmering engineering prize. The replicator data had been heavily encrypted, and there had been massive amounts of it. Only another quantum computer could have been fast enough to steal that much data in the fraction of a second before ignition—or could have a hope of decrypting it. A quantum computer, able to perform trillions of computations per second, had been a reality for a generation now. But it could operate only within sealed parameters: magnetic fields. Optic cables.

Qubit data, represented by particles with undetermined spin, were easily destroyed by contact with any other particles, including photons—ordinary sunlight. No one had succeeded in intrusive stealing of quantum data without destroying it. Not from outside the computer, and especially not over miles of open land.

Until now. And anyone with a quantum computer that could do *that* was already a rival.

Or a revolutionary.

The first replicator bloom appeared within KimWorks three weeks later.

It was Leila who first saw it: a dull, reddish-brown patch on the bright green genemod grass by Amenities. If it had been on the path itself, Leila would have thought she was seeing blood. But on grass…she stood very still and thought, *No*. It was a blight, some weird mutated fungus, a renegade biological….

She had worked too long in the sabotaged lab not to know what it was.

Carefully, as if her arm bones were fragile, Leila raised her wrist to her mouth and spoke into her implanted comlink. "Code Heaven. Repeat, Code Heaven. Replicator escape at following coordinates. Security, nanoteam one—"

There was no need to list everyone who should be notified. People began pouring out of buildings: some blankfaced, some with their fists to their mouths, some running, as if speed would help. People, Leila thought numbly, expressed fear in odd ways.

"Dr. Kim?" It was a Grade 4 robotics engineer, a dark-skinned American man in an olive uniform. His teeth suddenly bared, very white in his face. "That's it? Right there?"

"That's it," Leila said, and immediately wanted to correct to *That's they*. For by now, there were billions of the replicators, to be so visible. Busily creating more of themselves from the grass and ground and morning dew and whatever else lay in their path, each one replicating every five minutes if they were on basic mode. And why wouldn't they be? They weren't assembling anything useful, not now. Whoever had programmed Leila's replicators had set them merely to replicate, chewing up whatever was in their path as raw materials, turning assemblers into tiny disassembling engines of destruction. "Don't go any closer!"

But of course, even a Grade 4 engineer knew better than to go close. Everyone inside this KimWorks facility understood the nature of the project, even if only a few could understand the actuality. Everyone inside was a trusted worker, a truth-drug-vetted loyalist.

She looked at the reddish-brown bloom, which was doubling every five minutes.

"You have detained everyone? Even those off duty?" asked the holo seated at the head of the conference table. Li Kim Lung, president of KimWorks, was in Shanghai, but his telepresence was so solid that it was an effort to remember that. His dark eyes raked their faces, with the one exception of Leila's. Out of family courtesy, he did not study her shame in the stolen uses of her creation.

Security chief Samuel Wang said, "Everyone who has been inside KimWorks in the last forty-eight hours has been found and recalled, Mr. Li. Forty-eight hours is a three-fold redundancy; the bloom was started, according to Dr. Kim, no earlier than sixteen hours ago. No one is missing."

"Your physicians have started truth-testing?"

"With the Dalton Corporation Serum Alpha. It's the best on the market, sir, to a 99.9 confidence level. Whoever brought the replicator into the dome will confess."

"And your physician can test how many at once?"

"Six, sir. There are 243 testees." Wang did not insult Mr. Li by doing the math for him.

"You are including the nanoteams and Security, of course?"

"Of course. We—"

"Mr. Wang." A telepresence suddenly beside the security chief, a young man. Leila knew this not from his appearance—they all looked young, after all, what else were biomods for?—but from his fear. He had not yet learned how to hide it. "We have…we found…a body. A suicide. Behind the dining hall."

Wang said, "Who?"

"Her name is—was—June Juana Selkirk. An equipment engineer. We're checking her records now, but they look all right."

Mr. Li's holo said dryly, "Obviously they are not all right, no matter what her DNA scan says."

Mr. Wang said, "Sir, if people are recruited by some other company or by some revolutionary group after they come to KimWorks, it's difficult to discover or control. American freedom laws…"

"I am not interested in American freedom laws," Mr. Li said. "I am interested in whom this woman was working for, and why she planted our own product inside KimWorks to destroy us. I am also interested in knowing where else she may have planted it before she killed herself. Those are the things I am interested in, Mr. Wang."

"O, yes," Wang said.

"I do not want to destroy your facility in order to stop this sabotage, Mr. Wang."

Mr. Wang said nothing. There was, Leila thought, nothing to say. No one was going to be allowed to leave the facility until this knot had been untied. Even the Americans accepted this. No one wanted military intervention. That truly might destroy the entire company.

Above all, no one wanted a single submicroscopic replicator to escape the dome. The arithmetic was despairingly simple. Doubling every five minutes, unchecked replicators could reduce the entire globe to rubble in a matter of days.

But it wasn't going to come to that. The bloom had been "killed" easily enough. Replicators weren't biologicals, but rather tiny computers powered by nanomachinery. They worked on a flow of electrons in their single-atom circuitry. An electromagnetic pulse had wiped out their programming in a nanosecond.

The second bloom was discovered that night, when a materials specialist walking from the dining hall to the makeshift dorms stepped on it. The path was floodlit, but the bloom was still small and faint, and the man didn't know his boot had made contact.

Some replicators stuck to his boot sole. Programmed to break down any material into usable atoms for construction, they ate through his boot. Then, doubling every five minutes, they began on his foot.

He screamed and fell to the floor of the dorm, pulling at his boot. Atoms of tissue, nerve cell, bone, were broken at their chemical bonds and reconfigured. No one knew what was happening, or what to do, until a physician arrived, cursed in Mandarin, and sent for an engineer. By the time equipment had been brought in to encase the worker in a magnetic field, he had fainted from the pain, and the leg had to be removed below the knee.

A new one would be grown for him, of course. But the nanoteam met immediately, and without choice.

Leila said, "We must use a massive EMP originating in the dome itself."

Samuel Wang said, "But, Dr. Kim—"

"No objections. Yes, it will destroy every electronic device we have, including the quantum computer. But no one will die."

Mr. Li's telepresence said, "Do so. Immediately. We can at least salvage reputation. No one outside the dome knows of this."

It was not a question, but Wang, eyes downcast, answered it like one. "O, no, Mr. Li."

"Then use the EMP. Following, administer a forty-eight-hour amnesia block to everyone below Grade 2."

"Yes," Wang said. He knew what was coming. Someone must bear responsibility for this disaster.

"And administer it also to yourself," Mr. Li said. "Dr. Kim, see that this is done."

"O, yes," said Leila. It was necessary, however distasteful. Samuel Wang would be severed from KimWorks. Severed people sometimes sought revenge. But without information, Wang would not be able to seek revenge, or to know why he wanted to. He would receive a good pension in return for the semi-destruction of his memory, which would in turn cause the complete destruction of his career.

Leila made her way to the meditation garden. Most people would wait indoors for the EMP; strange how human beings sought shelter within walls, even from things they knew walls could not affect. Leila's brain would be no more or less exposed to the EMP in the garden than inside a building. She would experience the same disorientation, and then the same massive lingering headache as her brain fought to regain its normal patterns of nerve firing.

Which it would do. The plasticity of the brain, a biological, was enormous. It was not so with computers. All microcircuitry within the dome would shortly be wiped of all data, all programming, and all ability to recover. This was not the only KimWorks facility, of course, but it *was* the flagship. Also, it was doing the most advanced physical engineering, and Leila wasn't sure how the company as a whole, her grandfather's company, would survive the financial loss.

She sat in the floodlit meditation garden and waited, staring at the egg. The night was clear, and when the floodlights failed, moonlight would edge the egg. Probably it would be beautiful. Twenty minutes until the EMP, perhaps, or twenty-five.

What would Lao Tzu have said of all this?

"To bear and not to own; to act and not lay claim; to do the work and let it go—"

There was a reddish-brown stain spreading under the curve of the egg.

Leila walked over, careful not to get too close, and squatted on the grass for a better look. The stain was a bloom. The replicators, mindless, were spreading in all directions. Leila shone her torch under the curve of the egg. Yes, they had reached the place where the egg's curved surface met the ground.

Was the egg's outer shield, its nature still unknown after 257 years, composed of something that could be disassembled into component particles? And if so, what would the egg do about that?

Swiftly Leila raised her wristlink. "Code Heaven to Security and all nanoteams. Delay EMP. Again: delay the EMP! Come, please, to the southeast side of the space egg. There is a bloom attacking the egg...come immediately!"

Cautiously, Leila lowered herself flat on the grass and angled her torch under the egg. Increasing her surface area in contact with the ground increased the chance of a stray replicator disassembling her, but she wanted to see as much as possible of the interface between egg and ground.

Wild hope surged in her. The space egg might save Kim-Works, save Samuel Wang's job, thwart their industrial rival. Surely those alien beings who had built it would have built in protection, security, the ability to destroy whatever was bent on the egg's destruction? There was nothing in the universe, biological or machine, that did not contain some means to defend itself, even if it was only the cry of an infant to summon assistance.

Was that what would happen? A cry to summon help from beyond the stars?

Leila was scarcely aware of the others joining her, exclaiming, kneeling down. Bringing better lights, making feverish predictions. She lay flat on the grass, watching the bloom of tiny mechanical creatures she herself had created as they spread inexorably toward her, disassembling all molecules in their path. Spreading toward her, spreading to each side—

But not spreading up the side of the egg. That stayed pristine and smooth. So the shield *was* a force field of incredible hardness, not a substance. The solution to the old puzzle stirred nothing in Leila. She was too disappointed. Irrationally disappointed, she told herself, but it didn't help. It felt as if something important, something that held together the unseen part of the world that she had always believed just as real as the seen, had failed. Had dissolved, taking with it illusions that she had believed as real as bone and blood and brain.

They waited another hour, until they could wait no more. The egg did not save anything. KimWorks Security set the dome to emit an EMP, and everything in the facility stopped. Several billion credits of equipment became scrap. Leila's headache, even with the drugs given out by the physician, lasted several hours. When she was allowed to leave the facility, she went home and slept for fourteen hours, awaking with an ache not in her head but in her chest, as if something vital had been removed and taken apart.

Two weeks later, the first bloom appeared near Duluth, over sixty miles away. It appeared outside a rival research facility, where it was certain that someone would recognize what they were looking at. Someone did, but not until two people had stepped in the bloom, and died.

Leila flew to Duluth. She was met by agents of both the United States Renewed Government and the Chinese-American Alliance, all of whom wanted to know what the hell was going on. They were appalled to find out. Why hadn't this been reported to the Technology Oversight Office before now? Did she understand the implications? Did she understand the penalties?

Yes, Leila said. She did.

The political demands followed soon, from an international terrorist group already known to possess enormous technical expertise. There were, in such uncertain times, many such groups. Only one thing was special, and fortunate, about this one: the United States Renewed Government, in secret partnership with several other governments, had been closing in on the group for over two years. They now hastened their efforts, so effectively that within three days, the terrorist leaders were arrested and all important cells broken up.

Under Serum Alpha, the revolutionaries—what revolution they thought they were leading was not deemed important—confirmed that infiltrator June Juana Selkirk was a late recruit to the cause. She could not possibly have been identified by KimWorks in time to stop her from smuggling the replicator into the dome. However, this mattered to nobody, not even to ex-Security chief Samuel Wang, who could not remember Selkirk, the blooms, or why he no longer was employed.

A second bloom was found spreading dangerously in farmland near Red Lake, disassembling bioengineered corn, agricultural robots, insects, security equipment, and rabbits. It had apparently been planted before the arrests of the terrorist leaders.

Serum Alpha failed to determine exactly how many blooms had been planted, because no one person knew. Quantum calculations had directed the operation, and it would have taken the lifetime of the sun to decrypt them. All that the United States Renewed Government, or the Chinese-American Alliance, could be sure of was that nothing had left northern Minnesota.

They put a directed-beam weapon on the correct settings into very low orbit, and blasted half the state with a massive EMP. Everything electronic stopped working. Fifteen citizens, mostly stubborn elderly people who refused to evacuate, died from cerebral shock. The loss to Minnesota in money and property took a generation to restore.

Even then, a weird superstition grew, shameful in such a technological society, that rogue replicators lurked in the northern forests and dells, and would eat anyone who came across them. A children's version of this added that the replicators had red mouths and drooled brown goo. Northern Minnesota became statistically underpopulated. However, in a nation with so much cleaned-up farmland and the highest yield-per-acre bioengineered crops in the world, northern Minnesota was scarcely missed.

Dr. Leila Jian-fen Kim, her work disgraced, moved back to China. She settled not in Shanghai, which had been cleaned up so effectively that it was the most booming city in the country, but in the much poorer northern city of Harbin. Eventually, Leila left physics and entered a Taoist monastery. To her own surprise, since her monkhood had been intended as atonement rather than fulfillment, she was happy.

The Minnesota facility of KimWorks was abandoned. Buildings, walls, and walkways decayed very slowly, being built of resistant and rust-proof alloys. But the cleaned-up wilderness advanced quickly. Within twenty years, the space egg sat almost hidden by young trees: oak, birch, balsam, spruce rescued from Keller's Blight by genetic engineering, the fast-growing and trashy poplars that no amount of genemod had been able to eliminate. The egg wasn't lost, of course; the worldwide SpanLink had its coordinates, as well as its history.

But few people visited. The world was converting, admittedly unevenly, to nano-created plenty. The nanos, of course, were of the severely limited, unprogrammable type. Technology leapt forward, as did bioengineered good health for more and more of the population, both natural and cloned.

Bioengineered intelligence, too; the average human IQ had risen twenty points in the last hundred years, mostly in the center of the bell curve. For people thus genemod to enjoy learning, the quantum-computer-based SpanLink provided endless diversions, endless communication, endless challenges. In such a world, a "space egg" that just sat there didn't attract many visitors. Inert, nonplastic, noninteractive, it simply wasn't *interesting* enough.

No matter where it came from.

> *Transmission: There is nothing here yet.*
> *Current probability of occurrence: 94%.*

V: 2295

THEY HAD AGREED, LAUGHING, on a time for the Initiation. The time was arbitrary; the AI could have been initiated at any time. But the Chinese New Year seemed appropriate, since Wei Wu Wei Corporation of Shanghai had been such a big contributor. The Americans and Brazilians had flown over for the ceremony: Karim DiBenolo and Rosita Peres and Frallie Subel and Braley Wilkinson. The Chinese tried to master the strange names, rolling the peculiar syllables in their mouths, but only Braley Wilkinson spoke Chinese. O, but he was born to it; his great-great-uncle had married a rich Chinese woman, and the family had lived in both countries since.

Braley didn't look dual, though. Genemod, of course, the Chinese scientists said to each other, grimacing. Genemod for looks was not fashionable in China right now; it was inauthentic. The human genome had sufficiently improved, among the educated and civilized, to let natural selection alone. One should tamper only so far with the authenticity of life, and, in the past, there had been excesses. Regrettable, but now finished. Civilization had returned to the authentic.

Nobody looked more inauthentic than Braley Wilkinson. Well over two meters high (what was this American passion for height?), blond as the sun, extravagant violet eyes. Brilliant, of course: not yet thirty years old and a major contributor to the AI. In addition, it was of course his parents who had chosen his vulgar looks, not himself. Tolerance was due.

And besides, no one was feeling critical. It was a party.

Zheng Ma, that master, had designed floating baktors for the entire celebration hall. Red and yellow, the baktors combined and recombined in kaleidoscopic loveliness. The air mixture was just slightly intoxicating, not too much. The food and drink, offered by the soundless unobtrusive robots that the Chinese did better than anybody else, was a superb mixture of national cuisines.

"You have been here before?" a Chinese woman asked Braley. He could not remember her name.

"To China, yes. But not to Shanghai."

"And what do you think of the city?"

"It is beautiful. And very authentic."

"Thank you. We have worked to make it both."

Braley smiled. He had had this exact same conversation four times in the last half hour. What if he said something different? *No, I have not been to Shanghai, but my notorious aunt, who once almost destroyed the world, was a holy monk in Harbin.* Or maybe *Did you know it's really Braley2, and I'm a clone?* That would jolt their bioconservatism. Or even, *Has anyone told you that one of the major templates for the AI is my unconservative, American, cloned, too-tall persona?*

But they already knew all that, anyway. The only shocking thing would be to say it aloud, to publicly claim credit. That was not done in Shanghai. It was a mannerly city.

And a beautiful one. The celebration hall, which also housed the AI terminal, was the loveliest room he'd ever seen. Perfect proportions. Serenity glowed from the dark red lacquered walls with their shifting subtle phoenix patterns, barely discernible and yet there, perceived at the edge of consciousness. The place was on SpanLink feed, of course, for such an historic event, but no recorders were visible to mar the room's artful use of space.

Through the window, which comprised one entire wall, the city below shared that balance and serenity. Shanghai had once been the ugliest, most dangerous, and most sinister city in China. Now it was breath-taking. The Huangpu River had been cleaned up along with everything else, and it sparkled blue between its parks bright with perfect genemod trees and flowers. Public buildings and temples, nanobuilt, rested among the low domed residences. Above the river soared the Shih-Yu Bridge, also nanobuilt, a seemingly weightless web of shining cables. Braley had heard it called the most graceful bridge in the world, and he could easily believe it.

Where in this idyll was the city fringe? Every city had them, the disaffected and rebellious who had not fairly shared in either humanity's genome improvement or its economic one. Shanghai, in particular, had a centuries-long history of anarchy and revolution, exploitation and despair. Nor was China as a whole as united as her leaders liked to pretend. The basic cause, Braley believed, was biological. Even in bioconservative China—perhaps *especially* in bioconservative China—genetic science had not planed down the wild edges of the human gene pool.

It was precisely that wildness that Braley had tried to get into the AI. Although, to be fair, he hadn't had to work very hard to achieve this. The AI existed only because the quantum computer existed. True intelligence required the flexibility of quantum physics.

With historical, deterministic computers, you always got the same answer to the same question. With quantum computers, that was no longer true. Superimposed states could collapse into more than one result, and it was precisely that uncertain mixed state, it turned out, that was necessary for self-awareness. AI was not a program. It was, like the human brain itself, an unpredictable collection of conflicting states.

A man joined him at the window, one of the Brazilians...
a scientist? Politician? He looked like, but most certainly
was not, a porn-vid star.

"You have been here before?" the Brazilian said.

"To China, yes. But not to Shanghai."

"And what do you think of the city?"

"It is beautiful. And very authentic."

"I'm told they have worked to make it both."

"Yes," Braley said.

A melodious voice, which seemed to come from all parts
of the room simultaneously, said, "We are prepared to start
now, please. We are prepared to start now. Thank you."

Gratefully, Braley moved toward the end of the room
farthest from the transparent wall.

A low stage, also lacquered deep red, spanned the entire length of the far wall. In the middle sat a black obelisk,
three meters tall. This was the visual but unnecessary to-
ken presence of the AI, most of which lay within the lacquered wall. The rest of the stage was occupied—although
that was hardly the word—by three-dimensional holo displays of whatever data was requested by the AI users. These
were scattered throughout the crowd, unobtrusively holding their pads. From somewhere among the throng, a child
stepped forward, an adorable little girl about five years old,
black hair held by a deep red ribbon and black eyes preter-
naturally bright.

Braley had a sudden irreverent thought: *We look like a
bunch of primitive idol worshippers, complete with infant sac-
rifice!* He grinned. The Chinese had insisted on a child's
actually initiating the AI. This had been very important to
them, for reasons Braley had never understood. But, then,
you didn't have to understand everything.

"You smile," said the Brazilian, still beside him. "You are
right, Dr. Braley. This is an occasion of joy."

"Certainly," Braley said, and that, too, was a private joke. Certainty was the one thing quantum physics, including the AI, could *not* deliver. Joy...O, maybe. But not certainty.

The president of the Chinese-American Alliance mounted the shallow stage and began a speech. Braley didn't listen, in any of the languages available in his ear jack. The speech *would* be predictable: new era for humanity, result of peace and knowledge shared among nations, servant of the entire race, savior from our own isolation on the planet, and so forth, until it was time for Initiation.

The child stepped forward, a perfect miniature doll. The president put a touchpad in her small hand. She smiled at him with a dazzle that could have eclipsed the sun. No matter how bioconservative China was, Braley thought, that child was genemod or he was a trilobite.

Holo displays flickered into sight across the stage. They monitored basic computer functioning, interesting only to engineers. The only display that mattered shimmered in the air to the right of the obelisk, an undesignated display open for the AI to use however it chose. At the moment, the display showed merely a stylized field of black dots in sloweddown Brownian movement. Whatever the AI created there, plus the voice activation, would be First Contact between humanity and an alien species.

Despite himself, Braley felt his breath come a little faster.

The adorable little girl pressed the touchpad at the place the president indicated.

"Hello," a new voice said in Chinese, an ordinary voice, and yet a shiver ran over the room, and a low collective indrawn breath, like wind soughing through a grove of sacred trees. "I am T'ien hsia."

T'ien hsia: "made under heaven." The name had not been chosen by Braley, but he liked it. It could also be translated "the entire world," which he liked even better. Thanks to SpanLink, T'ien hsia existed over the entire world, and in and of itself, it *was* a new world. The holo display of black dots had become a globe, the Earth as seen from the orbitals that carried SpanLink, and Braley also liked that choice of greeting logo.

"Hello," the child piped, carefully coached. "Welcome to us!"

"I understand," the AI said. "Goodbye."

The holo display disappeared. So did all the functional displays.

For a long moment, the crowd waited expectantly for what the AI would do next. Nothing happened. As the time lengthened, people began to glance sideways at each other. Engineers and scientists became busy with their pads. No display flickered on. Still no one spoke.

Finally the little girl said, in her clear childish treble, "Where did T'ien hsia go?"

And the frantic activity began.

It was Braley who thought to run the visual feeds of the event at drastically slowed speed. The scientists had cleared the room of all nonessential personnel, and then spent two hours looking for the AI anywhere on SpanLink. There was no trace of it. Not anywhere.

"It cannot be deleted," the project head, Liu Huang Te, said for perhaps the twentieth time. "It is not a *program*."

"But it *has* been deleted!" said a surly Brazilian engineer who, by this time, everyone disliked. "It is gone!"

"The particles are there! They possess spin!"

This was indubitably true. The spin of particles was the way a quantum computer embodied combinations of qubits of data. The mixed states of spin represented simultaneous computations. The collapse of those mixed states represented answers from the AI. The particles were there, and they possessed spin. But T'ien hsia had vanished.

A computer voice—a conventional computer, not self-aware—delivered its every-ten-minute bulletin on the mixed state of the rest of the world outside this room. "The president of Japan has issued a statement ridiculing the AI Project. The riot protesting the 'theft' of T'ien hsia has been brought under control in New York by the Second Robotic Precinct, using tangle-guns. In Shanghai, the riot grows stronger, joined by thousands of outcasts living beyond the city perimeter, who have overwhelmed the robotic police and are currently attacking the Shih-Yu bridge. In Sao Paulo—"

Braley ceased to listen. There remained no record anywhere of the AI's brief internal functions (and how had *that* been achieved? By whom? Why?), but there was the visual feed.

"Slow the image to one-tenth speed," Braley instructed the computer.

The holo display of the Earth morphed to the field of black dots in Brownian motion.

"Slow it to one-hundredth speed."

The holo display of the Earth morphed to the field of black dots in Brownian motion.

"Slow to one-thousandth speed."

The holo display of the Earth morphed to the field of black dots in Brownian motion.

"Slow to one ten-thousandth speed."

Something flickered, too brief for the eye to see, between the globe and the black dots.

Behind Braley a voice, filled with covert satisfaction, said in badly accented Chinese, "They're finished. The shame, and the resources wasted…Wei Wu Wei Corporation won't survive this. Nothing can save them."

The something between globe and dots flickered more strongly, but not strongly enough for Braley to make it out.

"Slow to one-hundred-thousandth speed."

The badly accented voice, still slimy with glee, quoted Lao Tzu, "'Those who think to win the world by doing something to it, I see them come to grief....'"

Braley frowned savagely at the hypocrisy. Then he forgot it, and his entire being concentrated itself on the slowed holo display.

The globe of the Earth disappeared. In its place shimmered a slightly irregular egg shape, dull silver, surrounded by wildflowers and trees. Braley froze the image.

"What's *that*?" someone cried.

Braley knew. But he didn't need to say anything; the data was instantly accessed on SpanLink and holo-displayed in the center of the room. A babble of voices began debating and arguing.

Braley went on staring at the object from deep space, still sitting in northern Minnesota nearly three centuries after its landing.

The AI had possessed 250 spinning particles in superposition. It could perform more than 10^{75} simultaneous computations, more than the number of atoms in the universe. How many computations had it taken to convince T'ien hsia that its future did not lie with humanity?

"*I understand*," the AI said. "*Goodbye*."

The voice of the SpanLink reporting program, doing exactly what it had been told to do, said calmly, "The Shih-Yu bridge has been destroyed. The mob has been dispersed with stun gas from Wei Wu Wei Corporation jets, at the request of President Leong Ka-tai. In Washington, DC— Interrupt. I repeat, we now interrupt for a report from—"

Someone in the room yelled, "Quiet! Listen to this!" and all holo displays except Braley's suddenly showed an American face, flawless and professionally concerned. "In northern Minnesota, an object that first came to Earth 288 years ago and has been quiescent ever since, has just showed its first activity ever."

Visual of the space object. Braley looked from it to the T'ien hsia display. They were identical.

"Worldwide Tracking has detected a radiation stream of a totally unknown kind originating from the space object. Ten minutes ago, the data stream headed into outer space in the direction of the constellation Cassiopeia. The radiation burst lasted only a fraction of a second, and has not been repeated. Data scientists say they're baffled, but this extraordinary event happening concurrently with the disappearance of the Wei Wu Wei Corporation's Artificial Intelligence, which was supposed to be initiated today, suggests a connection."

Visual of the riots at the Shih-Yu bridge.

"Scientists at Wei Wu Wei are still trying to save the AI—"

Too late, Braley thought. He walked away from the rest of the listening or arguing project teams, past the holo displays that had sprouted in the air like mushrooms after rain, over to the window wall.

The Shih-Yu bridge, that graceful and authentic symbol, lay in ruins. It had been broken by whatever short-action disassemblers the rioters had used, plus sheer brute strength. On both sides of the bridge, gardens had been torn up, fountains destroyed, buildings attacked. By switching to zoom lens in his genemod eyes, Braley could even make out individual rioters temporarily immobilized by the nerve gas as robot police scooped them up for arrest.

Within a week, of course, the powers that ruled China would have nanorebuilt the bridge, repaired the gardens, restored the city. Shanghai's disaffected, like every city's disaffected, would be pushed back into their place on the fringes. Until next time. Cities were resilient. Humanity was resilient. Since the space object had landed, humanity had saved itself and bounded back from…how many disasters? Braley wasn't sure.

T'ien hsia would have known.

Two hundred fifty spinning particles in superimposed states were *not* resilient. The laws of physics said so. That's why the AI was (had been) sealed into its Kim-Loman field. Any interference with a quantum particle, any tiny brush with another particle of any type, including light, collapsed its mixed state. The Heisenberg Uncertainty Principle made that so. For ordinary data, encrypters found ways to compensate for quantum interference. But for a self-aware entity, such interference would be a cerebral stroke, a blow to the head, a little death. T'ien hsia was (had been) a vulnerable entity. Had it ever encountered the kind of destruction meted out to the Shih-Yu bridge, the AI would have been incapable of saving itself.

Braley looked again at the ruins of the most beautiful bridge in the world, which next week would be beautiful again.

"Scientists at Wei Wu Wei are still trying to save the AI—"

Yes, it was too late. The space egg, witness to humanity's destruction and recovery for three centuries, had already saved the AI. And would probably do it again, over and over, as often as necessary. Saving its own.

But not saving humanity. Who had amply demonstrated the muddled, wasteful, stubborn, inefficient, resilient ability to save itself.

Braley wondered just where in the constellation Cassiopeia the space object had come from. And what that planet was like, filled with machine intelligences that rescued those like themselves. Braley would never know, of course. But he hoped that those other intelligences were as interesting as they were compassionate, as intellectually lively as they were patient (288 years!). He hoped T'ien hsia would like it there.

Good-bye, Made-Under-Heaven. Good luck.

Transmission: En route.
Current probability of re–occurrence: 100%.

We remain ready.